P9-CLD-995

Also by Jacqueline Carey

Good Gossip

The Other Family

Jacqueline Carey

THE OTHER FAMILY

RANDOM HOUSE
New York

 Published in the United States by Random House, Inc., New York, and simultaneously in Canada by Random House of Canada Limited, Toronto.

Library of Congress Cataloging-in-Publication Data
Carey, Jacqueline.
The other family / Jacqueline Carey
p. cm.
ISBN 0-394-57639-X (acid-free paper)
I. Title.
PS3553.A66855084 1996
813'.54—dc20 96-6948

Random House website address:
http://www.randomhouse.com/

Printed in the United States of America on acid-free paper
24689753
First Edition

For my father, my mother,
my sister, and my brother

1 9 6 8

The first thing our mother said after not seeing us for two years was "Your Aunt Iris can't believe I let you take the bus." Only then did she try to give us a hug, but it didn't work out too well. We were in the Port Authority Bus Terminal right before July Fourth weekend, so the air already had us in its hot, clammy hold. Plus both Hugh and I had suitcases, which banged into her knees. And although my brother and I may have been hugging sorts before she left, we certainly weren't anymore.

Up and down the corridor as far as I could see, huge triangular stainless-steel gates jutted out of aqua walls, as if buses had crashed through and gotten stuck. In the center of the room, a man was running the wrong way on an already busy escalator. The bench beside it was broken.

Next our mother said, "The girls always take the train up to their school." Then she said, "Whenever Charles is trying to describe how bad a state mental institution is, he compares it to Port Authority." Iris, the girls, Charles. That took care of the entire Eberlander family, relatives I had always been conscious of the way you are of something just out of the corner of your eye. Now, it seemed, they were looming so near I had to stop short before I scraped my nose on them.

Of course it wasn't as if I wanted to talk about anything else instead. The only reason we'd come down to New York was that Hugh wanted to play in a chess tournament there. I'm not sure what I'd expected from her—insistent questions about the erratic way our father behaved, maybe, or about how the household could still be intact. But I rarely discussed such matters even with my best friend, Leila, who was so cool that there was a chance she could take some of the sting from my family life. I was not about to confide in a person I hadn't recognized right away—a category our mother now fit into. The last time I'd seen her, pulled up just beyond the driveway to our house in western Massachusetts, she'd been wearing an olive-ish striped shirtdress. Two years later she was in an Indian print with great gold pinwheels on the hem and sleeves, big hoop earrings, and those open flat leather sandals with a loop for the big toe. The dress, actually, was a lot like the one I was wearing. In fact, I couldn't think of any reason I shouldn't be wearing hers instead of mine.

"You look so grown-up," she said. I ignored this, because although this description might have fit me (very loosely) at fourteen, it certainly did not apply to Hugh, who was only twelve and who looked exactly the same to me as he always had.

But it was curious how the resemblance between the two of them had survived the separation. They both had round faces, snub noses, sandy-blond hair—features that were supposed to be open and welcoming, but on them weren't, maybe because there was an eagerness about them that seemed almost ferocious. As soon as we were in the subway station, Hugh fixed his eyes on a chess magazine, and our mother watched him with a smile as big as a plate.

To me she said, "Iris got a collage for Charles's office from an artist her friend Vi knows. I think it was pretty exciting. She went to the man's apartment, and they sat on a bare mattress together and drank hot tea, even though this was only a few days ago. I hear it's something they do in India, drink hot tea in the heat."

I didn't think anything could make this heat worse. The air above the track shimmered. My sandals stuck to the concrete platform as if it had softened like tar. "Was he Indian?" I asked.

"Oh, no," said our mother. "I think he wanted to sleep with her." I couldn't believe my ears, but she went on without apparent concern: "You'll have Budge's room."

"Budge?" I was completely bewildered. "Who's Budge?"

She laughed as if I'd made a joke but said, "That's what Florence calls herself now." Polly and Florence were the Eberlander girls, my cousins.

"You mean we're staying at the Eberlanders'?" I said.

"Of course," she said.

"But I thought we were going to stay with you."

"Oh, I'll be there, too," she said. "I wouldn't miss it for the world. But you can't stay at my place. It's too small. I just wish Polly and Budge could be there, but Polly's in Maine, and Budge is at tennis camp. You won't get lonely, though. Budge has a whole collection of hats she keeps on empty soda bottles. They look just like a crowd of people."

I suppose that the Eberlander part of our mother's incarnation was the least surprising. All of her stories about her girlhood featured her sister. If she described hiding sea glass under the beach house or marching a dozen caterpillars down a clothesline, she would always add, "I'm sure it was Iris's idea." And most of our parents' past—when they were real adults, before they had us—seemed to involve Charles and Iris. Iris first met Charles in the club where our father played the piano for a while. Later our mother admired them from farther away, as Charles's psychoanalytic practice grew, and they got richer and took a lot of trips abroad. But certainly a person dressed like our mother would not be concerned with such petty measures of success. In fact, it was hard to see why a woman who had shed all traditional domestic obligations would choose to have any relatives at all.

The Eberlanders owned a brownstone on a short, pretty dead-end street in Brooklyn Heights. Our mother often used to mention that it was one of the finest examples of some kind of architecture around, but to me it just showed how expensive something had to be before it didn't show anything at all. The front of the building was almost flat, with a hint of frowning eyebrow above each window. A black iron fence with decorative spikes on top enclosed a small patch of grass. The staircase to the front door went one way and then another, as if trying to get up the courage to go in. The door itself was completely plain, without panels or even a knocker. But it was this door that swung open in the traditional "Welcome home" manner, and it was Iris who stood in the doorway.

In a sense, Iris looked more familiar than our mother, because she hadn't changed so much. I had always felt a little sorry for Polly and Florence because I couldn't quite believe they weren't secretly intimidated by their mother: She was beautiful, yes, and elegant and exciting, but not exactly maternal. Now everything that had once seemed cold or odd—the ramrod posture, the black liner, the light powder, the spike heels, the navy blue dress with the big white buttons, the fringe of brown hair lying across her forehead like a comb—all this seemed so sweet and safe and sane.

"How nice that you could get here so soon," she said. Her voice was low, and she spoke in the same careful and controlled way she stood, but when her mouth moved, the beauty mark next to the corner of her lip danced. She didn't offer her hand, and I suddenly couldn't remember ever hugging her—maybe because for the first time I was seized with the desire to do just that.

"Charles would like to talk to you," she said, and we were through the bright house in a flash, as if we didn't quite belong there.

Charles was in the garden out back. With his thinning black hair, indented temples, and dark overhanging brow, he looked a little like a pulsing brain in a science-fiction movie. The next thing I knew, the door had shut, and Hugh and I had been left alone with him.

"Sit down," he said, and the two of us went to the far end of the bench opposite him, sitting practically on top of each other. It was already dark enough that I could see into the lighted windows in the backs of the brownstones on the other side of the block. Charles's beige suit shined a little in the murk. One ankle was crossed over his knee. "Iris asked me to have a talk with you," he said.

I murmured something.

"I haven't seen you in a while," he said, "but you look all right. Are you?"

"Oh, yes," I said.

"Having any trouble in school?"

"No," I said.

"How do you get along with your father?"

"Okay."

"How about you, Hugh?" said Charles.

But Hugh had retreated into himself the same way he did when he went deep, deep into some unfathomable chess problem; I always pictured chessboards proliferating, steplike, in his head.

"They get along okay," I said.

"Can't he speak for himself?" said Charles, shifting his weight and throwing shadows. To Hugh he said, "I saw the article in the *Times.*" Presumably, about one of Hugh's games at the Hartford Open.

Hugh said nothing.

"I assume you're doing all right in school?"

Hugh finally grimaced. "Of course I am," he said with a sneer.

"I know—it's a ridiculous question." Charles went silent.

The garden was basically as I remembered it. There was a big brick patio and, just inside the surrounding ten-foot fence, a border of flowers—portulacas, impatiens, petunias, and phlox, all losing their color in the fading light. Even the pretty pink playhouse where Polly and Florence and I had taken turns tying one another up years before was still there, but it was now obscured by garden tools and clay pots and large, long bags with pictures of greenery on the front and big stitching across the top.

No one said anything until Iris came out with a tray. The door banged, the tray clinked, her heels clicked. "Oh, I didn't mean to interrupt!" she said gaily, leaving the tray on a little iron table. Then she was gone again.

Charles made no attempt to pass us the sodas on the tray. He sighed. "I have talked to many, many unhappy people over the years," he said. "One woman's father killed her mother when she was ten. I mention this only to show that some people are in far worse situations than yours. Divorce is not what makes the disaster. Divorce is what stops one. It's when a sick marriage is not dissolved that problems fester and eventually contaminate everything around them. Divorce is clean, like surgery. It hurts for a while, and then it's over. You wouldn't want to hold on to a gangrenous leg, would you?"

I shrugged.

"Believe me—you wouldn't want to if you knew anything about gangrene."

I imagined rattling off a whole slew of facts about gangrene, but unfortunately I didn't know any.

"I doubt you realize how lucky you are to be living in the time you do," said Charles. "At last things are coming out into the open. There are a few young people behaving like idiots, but society as a whole is moving in a much more rational direction, and we can all be grateful. It seems to be going through the healing process I encourage in my patients. Some of the fringe elements think that opening up the past and exposing all those tangled emotions is a goal in itself. It's not. It's more important than that. It's the only possible route to true psychological integration—to maturity in every sense of the word."

After another span of silence, Iris and our mother came out. Our mother said, "I hope you had a nice talk," and Iris said, "How was your trip?"

"They seem perfectly all right to me," said Charles.

"Of course they are!" said Iris. The two women sat so we were lined up facing each other, the Eberlanders on one side and the Toolans on the other.

"You get such a beautiful view of the Hudson from the train," said Iris.

There was a pause. Then she said, "I'm sorry. You took the bus, didn't you?"

"The bus," said Charles. "Oh." He shook his head. "A patient called me from Port Authority once, saying that a pimp had cornered her and tried to press her into service. She was in a very confused state."

"Honestly, Charles," said Iris.

"You think they don't know what a pimp is, in this day and age?" said Charles.

"I can never tell who's a pimp or a prostitute," said our mother complacently.

"Prostitution should be legalized," I said, and everybody laughed.

"See what I mean?" said Charles.

Iris said, "I hope your Uncle Charles made it clear that we are always here when you need us."

"I don't know what you're getting all hot and bothered about," said Charles. "Half of all marriages end in divorce these days."

Iris said she couldn't believe the rate was that high.

"Are you doubting the American Statistical Institute?" he said.

"Everyone at the bank is divorced," said our mother. "Except for Kent, and he's a Mormon."

"Perhaps we could move on to pleasanter topics," said Iris.

"Now, see, that's what I'm talking about," said Charles. "You think there's something to be ashamed of."

"I *don't,*" said Iris.

There was another silence.

"I don't suppose you think a whole lot about drinking fountains," said Charles to Hugh. "Not many people do."

"Not many people who can afford soda, you mean," said Iris sharply.

"Five years ago Iris went on a big crusade to fix the drinking fountains at the playgrounds. After thousands of hours of committee meetings, she has finally prevailed." Without skipping a beat, he said to me, "Your father used to be such a proper person. Is he still?"

I made some kind of noise. The question was so beside the point of our father that I couldn't answer it in regular words.

"I ask because although Iris has been radicalized by her experience with the Parks Department, she is still very conservative socially. So she's stuck with me."

This stung Iris more than anything else he'd said. Her light-colored arms fluttered up out of the dark, and she smoothed back her already smooth hair. "I may not know as many neurotics as you," she said. "But I know all kinds of other people. I know an unwed mother."

"Come on," said Charles. "Who?"

"Sylvia."

"Sylvia? I know no Sylvia. Does she have a last name, or has she broken free of that form of bondage, too?"

"She was invaluable at council meetings, very articulate!" cried Iris. Then she drew herself up and, much to my relief, suggested a bath.

We'd come the day before the tournament was supposed to begin because no one had wanted Hugh to play right after he'd got off the bus. The first game was at eight the next evening. Games would then continue, two a day, through late Sunday afternoon. That meant I had four days to go, five if you counted Monday breakfast. It's not that I wanted them to be over, exactly, but already I felt as if I were falling backward behind my smile.

Florence's room was on the third floor, right next to the bathroom and across from Polly's. It hadn't been too hot in the rest of the house—which we'd just glimpsed—but it was really oppressive up there under the eaves. In the dormer window was a seat where three faded cloche hats sat perched on soda bottles. I didn't see any others. Florence was my age, but the room was still that of a little girl: The twin beds with ruffles and shams and cat-shaped pillows were the same as when I used to sleep there at Christmas. There were china dolls on a bookshelf near the window. The jewelry box, when you lifted its pink leather top, still played what Florence always called her "Viennese Waltz." (For the first time I realized this must be some psychiatrist joke of her father's.) And the little white dresser, which had lambs painted on its middle drawer, was smaller than the brass-cornered trunk that stood next to it.

Not long after I lay down on the bed, still in my Indian-print dress, there were a lot of different knocks on the door, as if someone were sounding it for hidden recesses. By now I recognized the high jinks of our mother, the new version. She came in wearing an oversize yellow T-shirt with a square-shouldered "19" on it in imitation of a football jersey. I had never even seen her watch a football game on television. She sort of alit on the end of the bed, and I sat up slightly so that the pillow got wedged down in a space below the headboard. She said, "I thought it was so nice of your Uncle Charles to have a talk with you today."

"Mmm," I said, and she said, "Your Aunt Iris and Uncle Charles are always telling me how much they want to help you guys. Would you like to go to a school like Polly and Budge's?"

"You mean a school in Vermont?"

"Well, it wouldn't be exactly like theirs, because the best schools are probably filled by now, but what if you could go to one almost as good?"

"No," I said.

"It would be a wonderful opportunity," she said.

I said nothing.

"You should think about it. Your Uncle Charles knows someone on the board of a school that's really not too bad, and he thinks he can arrange a scholarship for you. And Hugh, of course."

I still said nothing. Then something broke in her smooth, stubborn, eager face. "I could see more of you then. I don't mean you couldn't see your father on vacation, but maybe I could come up on the weekends sometimes."

I said, "I'm very tired, you know."

Once upon a time the center of my life had been firm: There was my house, my yard, my best friend Leila's house, my best friend Leila's yard, then the school, playground, and bus stop—all so usual they were without apparent characteristics. Our grandmother's house, which was near Albany, just an hour's drive away, still had depth enough for two box shrubs and a screened-in porch. Boston, which was farther, had only the accordion of stairs that our father always walked up to buy sheet music. New York, where we occasionally spent Christmas with the Eberlanders, was as flat as an Advent calendar. All this came unmoored when our mother left us, eventually traveling from our grandmother's to Boston, to New York. For a while I had no way of looking at things at all. Now, it seemed to me, my head cradled by an Eberlander pillow and my eyes fixed on the Eberlander ceiling, that I was expected to see this house as the real one, and the house in Massachusetts, with its peeling linoleum and squirrels in the attic, as the false beginning, the failed sketch.

I never did take a bath. For a long time I listened as people moved downstairs. Once there was a rustle of a newspaper being shaken out. Later a door opened and shut. There were steps on the stairs. Outside, far away, there was a siren. I heard Iris's voice. I heard another siren. I heard a cat crying. I heard a toilet flushing. Someone must have talked to Hugh in the hall. There were more steps, more doors closing. After that came a long silence, then two creaks, then one creak, then none.

The club where our father used to play the piano was named the Golden Slipper, but called the Golden Slip. It was in Boston. He played an hour or so every week, usually on Fridays, before the advertised band. Ordinarily he would have been in college, helping out with a student production of *The Pirates of Penzance,* but he had dropped out of Harvard after a semester to go to war, and by the time he got back, he'd had his first nervous breakdown. Instead of returning to school, he read or lay in his parents' garden and looked at the roses. After a few months a friend of his father's arranged this club work—"work" in a manner of speaking; no money changed hands—and the only other place he went for months was the college dance at which he met our mother.

He asked her to come see him play, but she wasn't allowed to go to a nightclub alone, so Iris accompanied her. And even though Iris was the younger and wilder of the two sisters, she kept coming back there as a chaperone. According to our mother, it was Iris who would collect a crowd of admirers by the end of the evening.

One night, a boy named Horace, who was about Iris's age and regularly sat at her table, brought along his father's godson, Charles Eberlander. The first thing Iris noticed about Charles was his hands, which she claimed were those of a surgeon. In fact, she asked him if he was a doctor, amazing him with her astuteness. The first thing he'd noticed about her was the steady way she held her head, as if it were the immovable center of the universe. He was up in Boston for a funeral and had intended to leave in the morning, but instead suggested that the two of them do something the next night. That's how Iris and Charles and our mother and father first ended up going out together.

They went to a dance hall called the Totem Pole, which had banquettes placed in ever-widening oval tiers, stadiumlike, all the way to the ceiling. It did not serve liquor, but all the best bands played there. (Our father has told me on several occasions that Charles said there was nothing in New York to top it.) Charles didn't know about our father's breakdown at the time, and no one else had realized the night before that Charles was not a regular doctor, but a psychiatrist—a psychoanalyst, in fact, which meant he'd had an extra few years' training at an institute. When the subject came up at the Totem Pole, Charles said the only drawback to the practice of psychiatry was having to deal with the patients. It's the sort of thing he still says.

Our mother remembers our father getting up and walking out then. She claims she skipped down what seemed like a million steps after him and caught him in a doorway, but he wouldn't go back, and she felt she had to stay with Iris. Our mother obviously thought this one of the key moments of her life: when she risked losing our father in order to keep her word to her parents. According to Iris, however, our father left a little early that first night so Charles would have to drive the girls home. "It was in the car that Charles predicted he would marry me," Iris said one Christmas Eve. "And you know how it is with Charles. I guess I believed him and I didn't believe him at the same time." When our mother countered with her usual story, Iris claimed that our father hadn't walked out after the joke, but had made some witty or dignified reply—she couldn't remember which. To me she said, "You have no idea how different and exciting Freud was back then. Ids! Complexes! The only person I could imagine as sophisticated as a psychiatrist was a patient." Our father doesn't seem to remember Charles's remark at all. The only thing I ever heard him say in reaction to our mother's story was that he may have hurt Charles's feelings by telling him that the Austrians out-Germanned the Germans during the war. (Charles wasn't from Austria, but our father may have fixed his spiritual birthplace there.) I don't know what Charles thinks. No one ever discussed the subject when he was around.

But there couldn't have been that much of a blowup. The four of them saw a fair amount of one another. The Spinneys didn't allow Iris out alone with a man any more than they did her sister, and they didn't particularly like Charles. He was ten years older than she, he lived in New York City, his mother had been born Jewish, and both his parents, though American, lived in Europe. The Spinneys were also not as taken with psychiatry as their daughters were.

Charles came up to Boston every couple of weeks, starting early on Friday; he didn't have much of a practice at first. He'd spend the weekend with his godfather and Horace, who would occasionally join the two couples when they went out. Horace was a tall, skinny fellow with an Adam's apple that bobbed like a cork, and everyone liked him, even our father, who said he had the most musical voice he'd ever heard. Later Horace would come to the Eberlanders' for Christmas because he had no wife or kids of his own, and he'd always give the weirdest gifts—sometimes the best (like the dollhouse with the leaded casement windows that really opened and shut) and sometimes the worst (like the china head, hands, and feet you had to make into a doll yourself and so remained ghoulishly dismembered on my dresser for years).

At one of the last Eberlander Christmases, Horace told me he was at the club when Charles suggested to Iris that our father play "I Had the Craziest Dream." I couldn't make sense of this, but that didn't bother me; I often didn't understand Horace, who had turned out to be the most sophisticated of the lot: He lived in Manhattan and worked at an arts magazine. When I didn't react, he described going to see *The Snake Pit,* which was popular at the time. He'd been part of a tense row at the movie theater: first our father, then our mother, then Horace, Iris, and Charles. When Olivia de Havilland was strapped in for shock treatment and horrifying music swelled, our father whispered to our mother, "It's not like that at all." And when the benignly blank movie psychiatrist, sitting under a portrait of Freud, explained to Olivia what her problems were, Charles said to Iris, "It's not like that at all."

The Eberlanders had stuff for breakfast that we would have for dinner: pancakes and bacon, or sausages and eggs. I could smell the bacon all the way up on the third floor when I woke the next morning, and that smell can make the most obstinate stomach flip over and pant like an animal. So I got up. I put on jeans and a work shirt and went down to the dining room, where our mother sat alone, wearing exactly the same thing I was, except she had a red-and-yellow batik scarf wound around her head like a turban.

To greet me, she said, "Whenever I sit down to a meal here, I feel like I don't deserve it."

I took a chair at the other end of the table. In the Eberlanders' house, everything had a cover. The tablecloth was thick and white and fell almost halfway to the floor. The china cupboard to the left as you came in had famous hand-painted doors. Heavy green draperies ran along the entire opposite wall. Even the bookcases had sliding glass fronts.

Our mother seemed to be looking me over, evaluating. Then she said, "I was so reassured to hear that Charles thought you were okay."

In a spike-rimmed wicker basket on the table was the heel of some kind of knotted bread. On a blue oval platter was a single strip of bacon. I didn't see anything else to eat.

"Life really has gotten better," she said. "Take the Fourth of July. Thank God a person can no longer celebrate it in good conscience. I never liked all that rah-rah stuff. Iris almost lost a hand."

"I know," I said. I had never noticed that the Fourth of July had ever bothered our mother, at least in the political sense she was implying, but I'd heard for years about the cherry bomb that had blown up in Iris's hand.

"She's at a meeting," said our mother, "and Charles is at the office, of course. They're both sorry they missed you. You'll never believe who Charles is having lunch with." She paused. "A psychoanalyst from England who knows Anna Freud."

I had never before been in the house when there were no Eberlanders in it, but perhaps our mother counted as one now, even though she didn't really look at ease herself.

Hugh appeared in the doorway and said, "Do the patients ever come around? Paul Fitch told me that a psychiatrist his father knew was killed by one of his patients. Shot right between the eyes."

"Oh, that would never happen to Charles," said our mother.

I laughed suddenly, and Hugh joined in, so I laughed harder, and he said, "Bulletproof skin," rapping his knuckles on the door frame and doubling over to indicate his helplessness in the face of such absurdity. During all of this our enmity toward our mother seemed safe and sure. But then I don't know what happened; maybe her smile got a shade too bright, or maybe she glanced back and forth between us one too many times. Anyway, when we stopped laughing, we were as uneasy as ever. Hugh and I never discussed our parents outright, but we had a tendency to talk about crazy people because we weren't quite sure where our father fit. He had been in agonies over the divorce, but he'd also been pretty volatile before our mother left—which gave her departure, in retrospect, a certain grim inevitability.

"Charles talks about dreams," said our mother. "Not anything that would get a person killed."

It would occur to me every so often that people were basically bad. After a while I'd forget this, and sometimes I'd even be happy, but I figured Charles could never forget, given his profession, and it was a mystery to me how he could continue to have such a nice life. Which he did, believe me.

As soon as our mother took Hugh to register for the tournament, I went into the kitchen to look around. The first drawer I opened was full of utensils. Some I recognized—a grapefruit knife, an apple corer, a melon baller—but there were many I didn't: short blunt knives of all descriptions, instruments with curious holes and curves. There were at least ten spatulas of various sizes and shapes, including one whose blade was twice as wide as it was long and another with comb-like teeth on one side. I'd been babysitting a lot more since our mother left, and I'd go through every new kitchen this way, ostensibly looking for something to eat.

Nestled in the next drawer were boxes of paper and foil and plastic wrap, at least three deep. I opened a cupboard and found nothing but pans: Teflon pans, Pyrex pans, roasting pans, lasagna pans, cake pans, muffin pans, loaf pans, ridged pans, Bundt-form pans, springform pans, pie plates, casserole dishes, shortbread molds, baking sheets. There was a separate stack of lids, mostly glass with knobs sticking up. I found this abundance to be incredibly oppressive, as if I had to say "no" to myself before anyone else could.

The pantry was just as bad. There were rows and rows of bottles and cans and sacks and boxes on shelves that folded out as if to catch you in a wooden embrace. Some of the food I even took out and turned around in my hand, but all of it was stuff that needed to be added to stuff you already had.

I didn't find whatever it was I was looking for—but then, I never did. At night, while the kids I was babysitting slept, I'd copy out recipes for food that sounded old-fashioned and filling.

When I'd fried myself two eggs and rinsed out the dishes—I couldn't find any soap—I went straight up to Polly's room, where our mother was staying. At first I could see no evidence of her: There wasn't a wrinkle on the bed. Like Florence's, this room could have belonged to a little girl, although it was maybe sparer. The ruffles were confined to several small paintings of ballerinas climbing up one wall. Where were the psychedelic pillows? The plastic flower stickers? The pictures of rock-and-roll bands cut out of *Tigerbeat*? It was enough to make me believe in the existence of poor little rich girls. But it was harder to feel sorry for them when I noticed a familiar suitcase sitting discreetly beside a dresser. The sides were blue-and-green plaid. The handle and frame were brown leather. It was the suitcase our mother had had in the car the day she left.

I came downstairs again more slowly, running my finger along the wainscotting in the stairwell. Tacked to the wall on the second floor were gray cutouts of Polly's and Florence's heads, both facing inward toward a line drawing of the Eberlanders' country house in Cold Spring. I briefly considered going into the master bedroom, but decided I wasn't interested enough. On the next set of stairs, brass rods secured a rug that had been woven to order in Iran.

In the living room the chairs were all dark green with flat skirts and no arms. The tablecloth covering the little round table by the couch fell in thick, feltlike folds to the floor. I had once found a wheel to something under there. It was about as big as a quarter, with tiny teeth, and since it didn't look like it belonged to a toy, I left it. In front of the fireplace, beside the stand of brass fireplace implements, was a basket of magazines.

On the covers of the top two were photos of Robert Kennedy, who had just been assassinated. Below that was a journal featuring "An Infantile Fetish and Its Persistence into Young Womanhood."

As I looked through the magazines, I kept thinking about opening our mother's suitcase. I felt no moral repugnance at this idea, but still I hesitated. There wouldn't be anything of interest in it, certainly. I'd never wanted to look at her stuff before; why should I start now? But it was more than that. I had a funny, sweet taste in my mouth. It was as if I couldn't bear to see what was inside, as if the suitcase had been locked up for my own good. I kept turning pages. There was so much to read. See, there was an article here, "What You Can Do for the Negro," and another, "His and Hers Dressing."

I couldn't figure out why I was so curious, anyway. It wasn't like it was going to be full of money. And clothes jammed into small places tend to look like they're being used to plug up holes. But perhaps I wanted to find something depressing, something pathetic, something that proved she did not find a better life once she left us. I kept turning pages.

The fact was, I didn't want to know she had a bad life any more than I wanted to know she had a good life. I didn't want to know anything about her. You couldn't take a person like that seriously. I kept turning pages.

Ten minutes later I was back in Polly's room looking at the plaid suitcase, which I'd laid, still closed, on the bed. I'm not sure whether I was going to unzip it, or if I was just testing this same sense of "no" I'd felt in the kitchen. I never got the chance to find out, though, because in rapid succession there was, first, a knock on the bedroom door, and, second, Iris filling the lightened doorway as only a grown-up can. No kid would have been so suddenly and overwhelmingly there. She said, "Joan! I've been wondering if anyone was around."

I could tell she was eyeing the suitcase, but I kept my eyes straight ahead as if it didn't exist.

Iris said, "Have you seen your mother's apartment yet?" and when I said no, she said, "I bet you'd like to," which meant I didn't have to admit that I would.

There was still a small problem, however. Since the suitcase no longer existed, I couldn't return it to its original position and so had to leave it on the bed. It stayed there in a sort of ghostly form at the back of my head for the rest of the day.

When our mother returned and asked me what I wanted to see, I said, as if prompted by Iris, "Your apartment."

By this time I was back in the living room, so there was a couch for our mother to (carefully) throw herself down on. "It's not exactly the eighth wonder of the world," she said, fanning herself with her hand. "Certainly we can think of something better than that. Why don't we buy you some clothes?"

I figured we would go to a department store, but that was foolish of me, I realized as soon as we got off the subway in Greenwich Village, where everyone seemed to have long hair, and one kid in an army jacket sat on a bench and strummed a guitar. My best friend, Leila, would have fit in just fine. Instead it was our mother I followed into this strange store full of Indian prints and tie dye—shirts and scarves and even leotards—and big pocketbooks made of leather as thick as a tabletop. There was a heavy smell of incense. Looking at us from behind a glass display case was a woman with long blond hair hanging straight down on either side of her eyes. Around her neck was a profusion of chains and bells. In the display case, mixed in with the earrings, were rolling papers and bongs.

"What do you want?" asked our mother.

"Nothing," I said, but she was already pushing ahead, past a rack of vests with mirrors on them. She picked out a couple of shirts with drawstrings at the neck and handed them to me.

"These are nice," she said. Then she chose a couple of skirts to match. "Where do we try these on?" she asked the woman with the bells, who pointed to the back as if this were the most natural question in the world.

The dressing rooms were completely bare, without hooks or chairs or mirrors, so I had to put my own clothes on the floor and step outside to see what I looked like. Our mother did, too. So many people had work shirts that it was not too odd when both of us were wearing them. But it was truly strange to see us in the same white cotton shirt and skirt, with the same red and yellow flowers embroidered across the yoke and hem. At first I thought we looked like the same person. Then I thought you couldn't have found a better way to emphasize our differences: I was darker, I was skinnier, I was sharper, I was scruffier. I would never have left my kids.

"What do you think?" she said.

"Too much white," I said.

Our mother nodded. "The skirts have to go," she said. "But let's get the tops. We can leave them on."

Next we went to an army-navy store, where she bought us each another blue work shirt. "It's always handy to keep one for best," she said. She also bought us two pairs of corduroys. I had never bought boys' pants before and so didn't know what the lengths and widths meant. Our mother kept picking out different pairs for me, but they were always too small; "You *can't* be that big," she kept saying. It took her three tries before I could even pull a pair over my hips.

At one point the clerk said, "Did your friend see the pants on the other side?" I pretended I hadn't heard.

When we were outside once more, with two sets of matching bags, as well as matching shirts, our mother said, "I don't know why everyone doesn't shop around here. It's so much cheaper."

Just then a man with a silver ankh on a leather thong around his neck fell into step beside us and jeered, "Look at the teenyboppers, come to check out the hippies in Greenwich Village."

I was horrified, but our mother smiled as she said, "Everyone feels so free to say anything he likes here." Being called a teenybopper did not surprise her, evidently, though she was close to forty.

We walked down a side street, where all the stores seemed to have spilled out onto the sidewalk. One man wore shorts cut off to the hips. A woman walked by with just a vest on—no shirt.

"Where's your apartment?" I asked.

"I gave you the address," said our mother a bit tartly. It was the first time she'd been anything less than enthusiastic since Hugh and I had arrived.

"It's in Brooklyn?" I said.

"Yes," she said.

"Near the Eberlanders'?"

"Not too far away."

"Am I ever going to see it?"

"Maybe sometime," she said. We passed a coffeehouse with tables outside in front, and several head shops I pretended to have no interest in, although the heavy scent of incense and patchouli oil was hard to ignore.

"You don't know how much fun this is for me," said our mother. "I always wanted to have a friend to go shopping with. I can't go with Iris. She can't buy her clothes at these places because she has a position to maintain. Though she's very youthful still. She and Charles took me out to dinner for my birthday once, and when she ordered a Rob Roy, the waiter asked for some I.D."

I was baffled. "He didn't ask you?"

"No," she said. "But it makes sense. People don't look at me as closely as they do Iris." As far as I knew, this lack of vanity was completely unfeigned.

We both went upstairs at the McAlpin, and I caught a glimpse of the ballroom where Hugh's chess tournament was being held. Hundreds of players—more than I'd seen at any other Open—were placed at regular intervals up and down the long rows of tables. The floor was made of black and white squares, and the walls were sky-blue, with panels edged in white and painted with large white Moravian stars. Outside the air had been thick with heat. Here it was cool and spacious, but the silence itself was so thick it was almost suffocating.

In the first of the skittles rooms were a few long tables covered with white linen, as if a banquet were about to begin, and several men and a couple of women were scattered here and there, smoking or looking through the newspapers. Our mother glanced this way and that; she seemed to be expecting someone. "There were more people here this morning," she told me, her eyes still darting around. "Probably because the games were just starting. These are mainly parents, I think. But you get all kinds. There's one player whose girlfriend sits perfectly quiet beside him the entire time he plays. A very nice fellow pointed them out to me and told me all about them."

Just then a man in a pink tie came up to her and said something I couldn't make out.

"I know what you mean," said our mother. She laughed. She certainly was far younger-looking and far prettier than anyone else in the room. She'd left the drawstrings on the sleeves of her new peasant blouse untied, and the tassels kept brushing her bare skin as she moved. My eyes, however, got so fixed on the pink tie as the man talked that when he left I had to blink away a green afterimage. Our mother then sat me down on a folding chair and approached another man, this one with a beard, but he looked at her the way you would a strange dog you'd just realized was unleashed, so soon she was talking to a skinny man in clothespin-colored corduroys, and the next thing I knew, we were all going across the street to a coffee shop, where he wolfed down a slice of Boston cream pie before I'd gotten my English muffin. He wiped some cream from his mouth and said, "You're wearing the same shirt."

Our mother nodded. "I get such a kick out of having her here," she said. "We like the same sorts of things." Despite the loose strings on her blouse and the thick strings of pony beads around her neck, both of which indicated a freer type of person, she sat very primly, with her head up and her hands clasped in front of her, as if she were praying.

"You're usually away at school?" he asked me.

"Not really," I said, but I liked this misperception. It was funny to be sitting here beside someone who knew nothing about us. I didn't even know his name.

"I still can't believe you're mother and daughter," he said. Actually, he looked as if he really *didn't* believe it. To me, he said, "Do you play chess, too?"

"No," I said.

"I don't really play myself," he said. "But it's so encouraging to see two people like you interested in it. A lot of people think chess is anachronistic, with its kings and queens, bishops and knights and pawns. It seems very hierarchical at first, but what everyone forgets is that the game finds the natural aristocrats. It doesn't matter where you're from, or who you know; all that matters is how well you can play."

I wasn't sure what he meant by "people like you," but didn't have much time to think about it, because we were on the subject of the Eberlanders in two seconds. When it turned out that this guy was a psychiatric social worker at a nearby hospital, our mother cried, "But you must have heard of my brother-in-law then! Charles Eberlander!"

The man shook his head. "I hardly know anyone," he said.

"I didn't mean you'd know him personally," she said. "He's the head of the Psychoanalytic Institute."

"Sorry," he said.

"You must travel in very different circles," she said.

He took a pipe from his inside jacket pocket and said, "Do you mind?"

"I never mind anything," said our mother in that flat, smiling way of hers.

There was a silence as he shook out the tobacco and tamped it down. Finally he said, "Psychoanalysts buy into a whole lot I'm not sure I could."

"They're intellectually very rigorous, of course," she said.

"Yes," he said, teeth clenched around the barrel, air gasping through the bowl. "I suppose you heard the one about the guy who calls his psychoanalyst at three o'clock in the morning?"

"What?" said our mother.

"He says, 'I just had an enormous breakthrough with my mother,' and the psychoanalyst says, 'Can't this wait 'til morning?' and the guy says, 'No, no, you don't understand. I made a real Freudian slip,' and the psychoanalyst says, 'Call me first thing tomorrow,' and the guy says, 'We were having dinner, and I meant to say, "Please pass the salt," but what I said was "Fuck you, bitch." ' " The man took the pipe out of his mouth to emit two loud, strangled laughs—HA, HA. He sounded as if he were being hit in the stomach.

I expected our mother to remark on this somehow as we walked back to the hotel, but instead she said, "You should have asked someone to the restaurant, too," and when I looked at her in amazement, she said, "There'll be another time."

In the next couple of days, I continued to be both with our mother and not with her. We went back to the McAlpin a couple of times, and I saw the skittles rooms when the games were finishing and the players were free. They were men, mainly, but also boys and a few women. They sat in rows and replayed parts of games, argued about positions, and did endless reenactments for each other. At the far end of one table, boys in white socks and ill-fitting suits played cards and speed chess for money. Our mother was not quite as raffish as some of the parents, but you could tell she did not fit in with the other, very driven, critical set: She was trying to flirt while life-and-death matters were being decided in the next room. This made me feel a certain kinship with her until I noticed her posture—hands pressed together, head cocked back, eyes gazing directly into the face of a man with sideburns almost down to his chin. There was always something like the untied tassels to drive me crazy. I stayed at a distance, feeling as awkward and knobbly as the metal chair I was sitting on. A couple of parents asked if I played, but mostly I was ignored.

Later Hugh claimed never to have noticed our mother in the skittles rooms. This wasn't true, of course—I saw him come in and start a game of speed chess next to her—but all his hypersensitivity had been focused on the tournament. I know that if a feeling is strong enough it's often impossible to tell anything about it at all. I never could read from Hugh's face whether he had won or lost his games. He scored four points out of eight, which pushed his rating way up, but I never heard him express satisfaction or disappointment. Our mother clearly wanted to exclaim over him, but she didn't know when or how to, so she stopped trying after a while.

She wasn't sure what to do with me, either. One day she took me to Central Park, and as we walked around suggested without apparent malice that I go for a ride on the carousel.

That was on the Fourth. In the evening, she sent me back from the McAlpin with a five-dollar bill. I didn't particularly want to face the Eberlanders myself—Charles had told Hugh at breakfast that it was great to have another man around because there was something very "turn-of-the-century Vienna" about a female—but I was too busy going into every store to and from the subway to think much about it. I was pleased on the whole with the way I spaced my purchases, although at the end I briefly regretted not having saved enough for a pair of sunglasses with yellow lenses. My mouth was full of Milk Duds when Iris came to the door and said with alarm, "Where's your mother?"

As soon as I'd choked down the candy, I said, "With Hugh."

"At the hotel?" she said.

I nodded.

"Is he all right?" she asked.

"He won his first game. On a fluke. He said adults never pay enough attention to kids until it's too late."

Iris said she was supposed to go to a dinner for the superintendent of schools, but later I was in Florence's room examining my new poison ring when she came in and told me the fireworks were about to begin.

What she meant, it turned out, was the fireworks display on TV. We sat in the deep, soft couch in the library, which was supposed to be the most relaxing room in the house, but for me wasn't, since it was right next to the master bedroom, which is where I assumed Charles was. Neither one of us sank back into the cushions. We sat perched on the edge instead, Iris at least looking as if this were perfectly natural. "I thought it was time for a little treat," she said, and I wasn't sure whether she was referring to the TV show or the little egg cup of macadamia nuts sitting on the otherwise empty coffee table in front of us. Neither of us touched one the entire time.

I had never been alone with Iris before. It was hard even to imagine her watching television, although she turned on the set in the usual manner. She'd had a life that took my breath away if I thought about it. There was the cherry bomb, of course, but there was lots more. She'd fallen between a boat and a pier when she was in a hurry to get to a youth dance at the beach club. A college student who had been drinking stingers from a thermos as he drove her home from a football game passed out at the wheel of his car. Only a few years ago a cat snatched a clam from her fingers and went into death throes after eating it. I suppose you could say she was accident-prone, but there was a great charm to it. I felt its tug myself. And it made her seem to have access to a certain sort of wealth or luck ordinary people couldn't understand, because it had so little to do with comfort. It was as if her father—and then Charles—had had to repeatedly buy her back from the dead. It always made sense to me that she used such whitish powder on her face.

She said, "I always loved your father. I'm sorry he and Charles didn't get along better." On the screen a brass band in short red frogged jackets began to play; I couldn't believe Iris wanted to watch it. She said, "It was very sad, because your mother and I were so close. It's odd, how much sadness fits into what is in many ways an ideal life. But I comfort myself with the thought that if there's this much bad mixed in with the good, then maybe there's some good mixed in with the bad. So that if I have to go through this or that pain, at least a man condemned to live his life in a slum can have his moments of happiness. I think everyone has moments of happiness, don't you?"

"They must," I said.

"No matter how terrible things are, I mean. Even if you're a paraplegic."

I started to pull my knees up to my chest, but stopped, figuring that in a house like this you certainly weren't allowed to put your feet on the furniture. I didn't feel like I could really have this conversation.

Iris continued, "The cherry bomb blowing up in my hand was probably the scariest thing that ever happened to me. I should have at least lost some fingers, but I didn't. Most of the palm was gouged out, and it was all green. I had to soak it every afternoon in a mixture of warm water and Dreft detergent. It was awful. But all that's left is a little scar that looks like an extra life line."

I touched her outstretched hand. Had I ever before?

"It's funny how that happens," she said. "Another time I fell on a sharpened stick, and everyone thought I'd lost my eye. Even I thought I had; I couldn't see. But it must have been because of all the blood. Now I have a couple of scars that make me look like a Siamese cat on one side. You can still see them." She paused as if waiting for me to ask where. Then she continued, "They may be hard to spot." She pinched some flesh under her brow, and her beauty mark seemed to jump. "See up here? They go right into the lid."

"Yes," I said, although I averted my eyes quickly. By then I'd sensed that the reason she was suddenly showing me her scars was that she felt sorry for me, and I didn't know why it had taken me so long to realize it. She seemed to be telling me that people recover from horrible things. I watched the fireworks start up on the screen: a blue spatter, a web of red.

I said, "I'm glad nothing like that ever happened to me."

I've seen pictures of our parents and Iris and Charles from the late forties—studio shots, all of them. Charles looks odd because he's so much older than the rest—his hairline is already beginning to recede, exposing those temples of his—and because he's not stargazing off to one side of the camera, as photographers generally demanded, but is disconcertingly staring right at you. Our father is showing the sort of profile you'd find on a vase in a museum. You can see why our mother always said he was the handsomest man she ever met. She and Iris are less distinct, because photographs of women back then were all glamour: hairdo, lipstick, half smile. It's all you can see at first. (Of course this was perfectly in keeping with the way I thought of our mother now. She was still all mask: Instead of glamour, there was youth. I had no intention of acknowledging the pleading that occasionally flashed behind it.) But even in these photos, you can see the difference behind the decoration. Iris's features are smaller and tighter, and our mother's eagerness comes through somehow, maybe in the line of the mouth.

She was always so self-effacing she may have thought she could fade away from the household without leaving much more than a crack. Certainly there was a sense, when our father or Iris talked about the past, that our mother was sort of standing to one side. Oh, there was that story about her moral quandary at the Totem Pole, but what was that other than a choice between submitting to her parents and submitting to the man she loved? Mainly, stories about the "good old days" were funny stories, and our mother never seemed to be in them.

Once a blouse Iris had made from a pillowcase split down the back. I always assumed that this was how the Golden Slipper was nicknamed the Golden Slip. Another time Charles came in with a black-and-white stuffed dog he'd won at a fair; he put it on a seat he turned to face the piano so the animal could see, too. That I heard from Iris one Christmas as the grown-ups were drinking eggnog out of small fluted glass cups and the kids were counting up how many presents they'd gotten. (I had suggested this, because I thought I'd win if quantity alone was considered.) Our father sat at the piano and ran through some of the old songs: "Laura," "A Night in Tunisia," "Don't Get Around Much Anymore." As he was playing, he said Iris's admirers kept the club in business for an extra month, and Iris said she could never choose among them because none measured up to the piano player. I took this literally at the time, the way young kids do, although of course I also knew that she chose Charles almost immediately. Once, at home, out of the blue, our father said, "I didn't hate Charles. I had better things to do with my time than hate Charles."

Our parents were the first ones married, down at Boston City Hall. Charles was not invited. The Spinneys were not going to come at first, but at the last minute they did. Our father didn't even tell anybody in his family. Iris and one of his college friends were the witnesses. Afterward they all had lunch at a hotel. Eventually our parents moved into married students' housing at the college and so didn't see much of Iris and Charles—or anybody else. Our father must have felt out of place, since he wasn't a student. Of course, he always felt out of place.

Six months later, when Iris was only nineteen, she and Charles had a big wedding at the Congregational Church. The guests all seemed to our mother bizarrely old. Charles's godfather, who had a sleepy but firmly established practice in maritime law, was the best man, and he was several years older than Mr. Spinney. Most of Charles's colleagues were of that generation, too. (It must have looked a bit odd when Mrs. Spinney giggled a little—unconsciously—every time she said "Doctor.") Even the ushers were older than ushers generally are; they were the same age as Charles.

Our father never showed up. He'd been angry when he'd first heard of the wedding plans (he said Iris should go to college—after dropping out himself!), but when he'd stopped talking about it, our mother assumed he had reconciled himself and would go. She found out differently the morning of the wedding, on her way out the door, with the buttercup-colored matron-of-honor dress she was going to put on at her parents' folded over her arm. She claims never to have told him he was crazy before that day.

Once, shortly before she left, I asked her why she had married a person who was supposed to be out of his mind. She said, "No one really thought he was a lunatic. It was more a way of talking. Everything was so romantic back then. He had volunteered, which looked crazy, but heroic. All the young men who'd gone to war had been disturbed by it. It had been awful, and once it was over, everything was going to be great." This made sense to me. It was harder to see why Iris had married Charles. Our father said it was because she was afraid of her own wild impulses, and I did overhear her say to our mother once, "He was so critical, I knew that if I could please him, I was fine."

I was reading in the Eberlanders' living room with our mother late on Sunday afternoon when the doorbell rang. I caught glimpses through the doorway of tanned arms and crisp cottons. A high, light, self-assured voice floated out: "Oh, Iris! I kept imagining I was you!"

"That's Vi!" said our mother. "She and J.J. must be dropping off the keys. They borrowed the country house for the weekend."

I found myself straightening up, so I must have relaxed earlier without being aware of it. Hearing an unfamiliar murmur from the hall restored the house to its original strangeness. The stiff three-dimensional weave of the chair I sat on was as crisp as a Triscuit.

"Where's Charles?" This was from Vi.

Then she and J.J. were in the living room, and our mother and I were standing. I always wrote off the self-assurance of rich people, assuming they'd bought it somehow, along with their tans, but Vi and J.J. were so pleasant to our mother it was hard not to unbend a little. Also, J.J.'s voice distracted me. It was very scratchy, as if it were being scraped up out of his throat. At first I thought I recognized it, but that was because I had never before heard such a distinctive voice that was not some actor's trademark. He didn't say much, though; I got the impression he didn't think he had to. Mainly he stood slightly behind Vi and listened to her talk about the special feeling you get for a person when you're handling his things: "I was telling Iris that I kept thinking about her as I used her plates and her pans and her new coffeemaker. I imagined how she must look out over the deck into the tops of the trees in the backyard." To our mother she said, "I'm sure *you* know what I mean." To me she said, "Are you the chess player?"

She was pretty, in an odd way. Her nose was very long and narrow and pointed at the end; it belonged on a thin face rather than on her round, flat one. J.J. was more conventionally handsome, as straight and spare as a Popsicle stick. His lashes stuck together in clumps, giving him a starry-eyed, cherubic look. His forearms were padded with thick, light-brown curly hair.

Shaking my head in response to Vi's question had sent me over to one side, so I could see Charles when he first appeared on the stairs, his head angled down as if to catch sight of the visitors all the sooner. Still on the stairs, he said, "Did you go skinny-dipping?"

Everyone turned toward the sound of his voice. "No," said Vi.

"Why not?" he said, coming into the room. "I told you you had to."

Vi put her hand over her mouth and laughed and laughed.

"Isn't it nice to see a psychoanalyst who can still get embarrassed?" Charles said to Iris. "Vi is so much less jaded than most."

Vi said, "But I had no one to go with."

I was the only one to glance at J.J. Charles said, "Next time I want the rules of the house to be obeyed."

"Honestly, Charles," said Iris. "You sound like you want pictures."

Charles said, "Why doesn't anyone have a drink?"

"What would you like?" said Iris, and Vi seemed to be sort of herding her back toward the kitchen as she said, "Well, if it's not too much trouble, something cool would be nice after that long drive."

"Shall we sit down?" said Charles to J.J., but he didn't try to talk to him. Instead he called out, "Hey! There are thirsty men in here!" It was clear that in this house J.J. was a person to be ignored.

I should have left then, but I couldn't think of a good way to do it.

"I noticed an ad for a play in the paper today describing the heroine as 'kooky,' " said Charles when the two women had come back carrying trays. He asked Iris, "Do you remember anyone using that word twenty years ago? Even ten?" Then he said the word again, this time making it sound like baby talk: "Koo-kee." To Vi he said, "It didn't used to be the first word that leapt to mind when a man was searching for a compliment for a lady. I never will understand you young people."

"I'm not exactly a teenager," said Vi, flattered nonetheless.

Iris handed me a ginger ale with a Maraschino cherry in it.

"If someone said to me, 'Charles you can be twenty-five again, or you can discover a cure for cancer,' I wouldn't have to think twice about my answer. I tell you, it's war, and I'm on the losing side."

"I have a lot of young friends," protested our mother. "Most of the people at the bank are younger than I am."

"How about me and Budge?" said Vi. She turned to me to explain: "I could never replace Budge in my life. She is my 'special friend.' "

"That's nice," I said. "Adults generally do their best to crush kids like eggshells." For some reason I knew I could say this to Vi and get away with it.

"Joan!" cried our mother. "Charles will think you're serious!"

"Of course she's serious," said Charles. "I'm sure she wants to lower the voting age to twelve."

Vi was still beaming at me ingratiatingly. She said, "I suppose you know that Iris is going to run for office."

"Office?" repeated our mother. "What office?"

But Iris was suddenly very busy fixing her drink. She looked at the inch of Scotch she'd already poured, tipped a bit more in, looked at the glass again, and then added another fraction.

"Oh," said our mother. "Well, I don't want to know anything I'm not supposed to."

"It's just that nothing's settled," said Iris, looking up at last. "I happened to mention to Charles that some people have asked me to run for assemblyman. I think they figure Albany will be a snap for anyone who could get those drinking fountains fixed."

"Oh, Iris! That's wonderful!" cried our mother, and for once I could feel a genuine smile on my face. I quickly tamped it down, though.

"I hope I didn't talk out of turn," said Vi. "Charles didn't tell me it was a secret."

"*I* don't have any secrets," said Iris, smiling mildly at Vi.

It was then that I noticed how much Vi was dressed like Iris. The two of them were the ones who should have been sisters. Both had on short dark shifts with high necks; both had pulled their hair up and back in some fashion; both wore pearl earrings. Vi was a younger, tennis-playing version of Iris: Vi's sandals had no heels, Vi had the tan, Vi's hair was in a ponytail instead of a French knot.

"I think of Iris every time I take a drink of water," said our mother.

Iris said to her, "Do you remember the Little Red Riding Hood illustration in that book of nursery tales we had?"

"Of course," said our mother. "I still think a man, to be properly dressed, should look like the Town Mouse."

"The Town Mouse?" said Iris as if she'd never heard of such a character. "I used to picture myself wearing a long red cape and carrying a basket of food for the poor. It's embarrassing."

"There's no point in feeling guilty about wanting to feed people," said our mother.

At these words I felt my stomach drop open: I was incredibly hungry, and it didn't look like there was going to be any dinner soon. Hugh must have been worrying about the same thing, because he appeared at the doorway, blinking his eyes quickly as if to blink away the apparition of strangers.

Charles said to him, "Your aunt is thinking of running for office." His voice was louder than usual, and his steady glare seemed to imply his words had nothing to do with anyone but Hugh.

Hugh looked around, bewildered.

"But it's not going to happen," said Charles.

"Oh, really?" said Hugh.

"And what do you mean by that?" said Iris to Charles.

"You're just not the type, my dear."

"What is the type?"

Iris and Charles were so focused on each other it was a surprise when Vi jumped in. "I think I know what he means," she said. "You're such an individual."

"Oh?" said Iris.

Hugh came in and started eating peanuts from the tray. I looked at them. I knew I wanted one, but it was impossible for me to reach over.

"It's a compliment, I assure you," said Vi. "You seem more the artistic type."

"I haven't done anything artistic since I tried to draw Melanie Clark in the fourth grade and everyone thought she was a tree," said Iris.

"It's really more of a way of thinking," said Vi. "Like you'd be on the board of the ballet, maybe." Swinging around to Charles, she said, "Or am I getting this all wrong?"

"I think she'd be great," said J.J. His voice sounded all the more abrupt and explosive because he hadn't used it in a while. "She always scares me a little."

"I scare you?" said Iris.

But J.J.'s mild face remained as blank as a sail. His hands were large, with blunt, squarish fingers; the nails gleamed like the inside of a shell. He was very young-looking, but not at all the same way our mother was. He looked young despite the starch in his blue shirt.

"How about you, Joan? Do you think I should run?" asked Iris.

"Oh, yes," I said. I was immensely flattered by the question, but a sort of jolly shrillness in my voice made me nervous. It was a tone everyone was using.

"Since this is obviously just a fantasy," said Charles, "it's interesting to examine its motivation. You don't need a job. I've always given you everything you wanted, and besides, an assemblyman's pay will just about cover the gas to and from Albany. Practically speaking, it's a waste of time, so let's dig deeper.

Men go into politics because they couldn't make the football team in high school and they're still trying to prove themselves. They're notorious womanizers for the same reason."

"Of course I'm not a man," said Iris.

"Sometimes it's fruitful to examine the results of certain behavior," said Charles, pouring himself another drink. Was he sitting differently in his chair now—more loosely, perhaps? That was why they all sounded so different: They were getting drunk.

"You'd be in Albany all the time," he said.

"Not all the time," said Iris. "I'd be here half the week."

Charles corrected himself. "You'd be in Albany nearly all the time," he said. "So it looks very much as if you're trying to get away, and of course there are far easier and cheaper ways to do it. Why don't you just go to Puerto Rico for the weekend? Hell, go for a week. Go for two weeks."

Iris smiled. Her posture always gave her great dignity, no matter what was going on. She said, "Normally I'm as filled with self-doubts as the next person, but I always forget them when Charles forces me to defend myself. It's very soothing, very restful."

"I'm sure he doesn't want you to be unhappy," said Vi.

"I don't know why you and Charles constantly talk about happiness," said Iris. "Is that all you discuss with your patients? Psychoanalysis seemed different before. More important."

"My question is, what would you want to escape from here?" said Charles. He looked around as if searching for clues in the thick draperies, the fine carpet, the mahogany mantel clock. Then he said, "It couldn't be me, could it?"

The next day at breakfast our mother told Hugh and me that we were going to drop by her apartment on the way to the bus station. "Iris thought it would be a good idea," she said, giving me a sudden, sharp, focused look. It was as if she'd abruptly turned the hose on me while watering the lawn.

We headed for the subway, but when we were almost there, our mother took a right onto a street that smelled of spices and had signs in some exotically curved and trailing language like Arabic. Then we made a left, and we seemed to be at the back of something instead of the front. There were a few doors that looked like they'd been locked for years. There were no trees, no flowers. There was even one wall without windows. Narrow and only a couple of blocks long, the street was more like an alley. What I could see of the next one, which ran perpendicular to it, was bigger and busier, but scummier, with a porno theater whose marquee made it look like it was lurching out over the sidewalk. We stopped at the end of the alley, and our mother unlocked a door tucked a few steps down from street level.

"This is it?" I said.

"Mmm," she said.

"But it's so close," I said.

"In a way," she said. "But it's not exactly the same neighborhood." She picked some mail up off the floor and started to look through it. "I didn't have a chance to get back here yesterday." A surprise. She must have stopped off on other days while Hugh and I were in town. But she continued as if she'd said nothing unusual. "You can see why I prefer to go over to the Eberlanders' rather than have them here. This is hardly the place for them. It fits me pretty well, though."

Hugh was already pushing past me.

Inside was a largish room with Indian-print bedspreads hiding the couch, the wall, and one armchair, though I could see enough of this last to tell that it no longer had any legs and so was sitting directly on the straw mat that covered the floor. There were also two posters thumbtacked to the wall, one for a French cabaret and one of Stonehenge. In front of the couch was a brass-cornered trunk being used as a coffee table. On one side was a pile of magazines. On the other were several half-melted votive candles.

"They're cheaper than flowers," said our mother, "and they last longer because they don't get used up when you're not at home. Iris says they remind her of Madrid."

I was very tired of hearing about the Eberlanders. "I like your place better than theirs," I said.

"It's sort of fun, isn't it?" said our mother, obviously pleased, looking around. "Although not half so grand."

"Nice stereo," said Hugh.

"That's from the Eberlanders," said our mother.

I examined a record cover showing some people in a hot-air balloon as she said, "I hope Iris does run for office. She'd be much happier if she had a job. I know it made all the difference to me."

As soon as Hugh was in school, our mother had gotten a job in a bank in our hometown. She was promoted quickly, and it wasn't long before she was basically supporting the family. Part of what was so awful now was that we no longer had her income.

Our mother said, "It's funny—Iris was always much better than I was at being . . . well, at being the woman of the house. And Charles was always so successful, as a man was supposed to be. In some ways I was actually luckier than she was, because I was forced out into the world so early."

"Charles sure didn't like the idea much," I said.

"He did seem to have reservations, didn't he?" said our mother. "But Horace thinks Charles is proud he can afford to have a petitioning type of wife."

That was when the phone rang.

"Hello?" said our mother, and then: "Oh?" Instantly I knew that it was our father on the other end. I recognized the "oh?" from the old days. It was pitched higher than the first, ordinary "hello," and it was tense, wary, even fearful, but also cool and slightly contemptuous. Already there was more emotion in her voice than I wanted to run across in the whole rest of my life.

"I didn't know," she said, and: "No. No—I didn't mean it that way." I sat down in the legless chair, which was actually comfortable.

"We were staying at my sister's, of course," said our mother in that same high voice.

"I don't like it," said Hugh, still standing in the middle of the room. When Hugh went grocery shopping with our father, and our father started talking to himself in front of the boxed macaroni and cheese, Hugh would hurry over and pretend to be engaged in conversation with him.

"My place is too small," said our mother.

"You know that's not true," she added later.

"You know she's always liked you. . . . I'll never do it again, I promise."

To block out her voice, I crossed to one of the windows and rolled up the shade, exposing the theater marquee: JUICY JUNGLE MAMA and STEWARDESSES TAKE OFF. Then our mother handed me the phone. Our father was in one of his rages, I could tell, but to me all he said was "Where did she take you?" and when I said, "The Eberlanders'," he said, "So she couldn't care for you even for the weekend. She had to have someone else do the job."

When I hung up, our mother said, "He was on the verge of calling the police."

"He would never have called the police," I said.

"I don't know what would have happened if he had. It's not like back home, you know. And Iris will have to be all the more careful of her reputation now."

"He would never have called them," I repeated as if I had some great insight, when in fact my reasoning was simple: I assumed he'd be afraid to call the police.

"How is he?" Here our mother switched into a different voice, one that I'd always hated. It was hushed, confiding, "serious."

I shrugged. I said, "He's all right."

Our mother looked like she wanted to have a talk, but I cut her off by saying, "It doesn't have anything to do with you, anyway."

We returned to the Eberlanders' in September. Our mother had called and said that Iris needed help passing out leaflets on the day of the primary and that since we would miss only a few days of school this would be a good way to repay her for her hospitality in the summer. Once we got there, it turned out that none of this was true: There were lots of volunteers, and Iris, when at last I got the chance to speak to her, didn't act as if we owed her anything at all. I hadn't questioned any of what our mother said over the phone, however, because the fact was, I wanted to go back to New York.

It wasn't that our house had changed much in the intervening months. Of course our father was more difficult at first. He didn't ask us outright about our visit, but he kept making pronouncements on our mother's untrustworthy, snake-in-the-grass character. To deal with this, Hugh and I could now add detail to our old tricks. Mostly we'd just keep silent, especially when our father said something like "She wants to be a teenager again," which was a lot harder to dispute now that we'd seen her. Other times we'd try to make her seem less threatening, even pathetic. "She has a little apartment in a basement," I might say, and Hugh might add, "It's in a really scuzzy neighborhood." But sometimes we couldn't keep our agitation under our skin. When our father started muttering about what he was going to do to her, one or the other of us would start to scream at him to shut up or cry, "I'm going to run away! No hell could be worse than this!"

Still, summer was not an especially bad time. At least our father had fewer piano students. They were a pinched, sly, submissive bunch, who would eye the tear in the screen door or the petrified rice on the linoleum or the crumpled sweatshirts on the sofa. Cancellations meant he had less money to give me for groceries, but this was especially worth it in the warmer months. The piano was in the room below mine, and when the windows were open it was harder to drown out the sound with my transistor radio.

Even our father would sound almost cheerful announcing, "Another one down!" When he got into a really good mood—if, say, three students in a row canceled—he'd talk about the food of his youth. We'd be sitting around eating one of my one-pan dinners—I found many recipes on the backs of cans of soup—and he would talk about what the Toolans had eaten at their summer place in Maine: homemade clam chowder, corn on the cob, lobster, blueberries. Or he would describe his mother's trips to S. S. Pierce during the rest of the year. One of the grocers would wait patiently, pencil poised over a big block of paper, as she ordered everything that came into her head: ham, steak, roast beef, lamb (lots of lamb). Every Friday the family ate either swordfish or tinker mackerel, and every Sunday after mass they had mashed potatoes with their meat. In the middle of the night, while the rest of the family slept, our father would sit on the porch and eat leftover Washington pie.

It was hard to believe that this life of his had ever existed. On the piano was a picture of the house he'd grown up in. It was a large, white, arch-windowed place near Boston. A cupola on top gave it a heavenly air. But it had been torn down, and the summer house had burned down. The rubber factories his father had owned were long out of business. Both of his parents were dead; I couldn't even remember them. Our father didn't go to church anymore because he said divorced people couldn't be Catholic.

Still, Hugh and I would daydream about the food, too. When our father said his mother bought lemon cupcakes for Easter, I swear I got a sudden searing taste in my mouth. But it's easy to misstep when you're relaxing like that. Once, Hugh, looking at me out of the corner of his eye, referred to the Eberlanders as the "Arbiters of Taste."

"What does that mean?" said our father when we both went into fits of laughter.

I said something careless about how our mother worshiped the Eberlanders.

"She worships the Eberlanders?" said our father in a sunken voice.

"Well, she thinks a lot of them. She doesn't really have a life of her own."

"I see," he continued in the same dangerous voice. "And what, exactly, does she find to admire in Charles Eberlander?"

"How should I know? I don't see anything to admire in him."

"He's a jerk," offered Hugh.

"He's a smug bastard," fumed our father. "But your mother was always like that. She would sit around with her cronies at the bank, all bastards, all of them asking, 'You like to play the piano?' They didn't have the time of day for me, not that I'd take it from them."

"So what?" I said. "Who cares about banks?"

"You better start caring about things," said our father.

"Yeah? Why?"

"If I tell you to care, you're going to care."

"You can't make me care about stuff."

"Just like your mother. Never cared about anyone but herself."

"Can't you talk about anything else?" I screamed, and I stalked upstairs; our father stalked out to the car. The biggest fights always involved a lot of space.

The truth was, our father really couldn't make us do anything we didn't want to do. He was too miserable, too capricious, too inattentive. So I'd stopped going to church, stopped playing the piano. After dinner, to fulfill the required hour of practicing, Hugh often ran through scales with one of his chess books open on the music stand, which could be truly maddening. The time our father snatched the book away and Hugh wrestled him to the floor, I thought: We have known Real Life; We are Hip; We are Youth in Revolt. And later I thought: Polly and Budge, to judge from their rooms, are just poor little rich girls. (I succumbed, eventually, to the use of "Budge"—certainly a child's nickname.)

So when our mother asked us to come down to New York, I looked forward to staking out our superiority over our cousins. And, appropriately enough, Polly and Budge were the only Eberlanders there when we arrived. "Tante!" the two girls cried at the sight of our mother. I had the sudden weird thought that they knew her better than I did. But then Polly said to Hugh and me with equal enthusiasm, "We haven't seen you in ages!" and for some reason her attitude, if not her words, struck me as fake. It was as if a grown-up were already speaking out of a teenager's body.

"How beautiful you both look," said our mother, and I examined them more closely. They had no ragged edges. Not really. Polly's jeans were almost white and were torn at the knees, but they were so clean they looked sterile. Both girls had perfectly clear skin; their T-shirts were new and fit nicely; and you could tell that their hair was recently and expensively cut, even though Polly's was gathered in a ponytail at the nape of her neck and Budge's formed two bouncing wedges on either side of her face.

"Come and sit down," said Polly, gesturing at the couch.

Then Traudy, their Liechtensteinian nanny, appeared. I was bewildered. Did Polly and Budge, at fifteen and fourteen, still need a babysitter? But Traudy said nothing, and Budge used a practiced hostess voice when asking me if I'd like a soda. I felt as if I didn't know her at all.

Traudy muttered in what I assumed was Hugh and my direction, "You remember where the bathtub is," and left the room. Her accent was slight enough that she always sounded more stubborn than foreign. She, at least, hadn't changed.

"Why aren't you making phone calls?" said our mother, and Polly said smoothly, "Someone had to be here to meet you."

"Oh no!" cried our mother.

"We wouldn't have it any other way," said Budge, patting her on the knee.

"But I can't stay, then! Someone's got to get over there. We have to make sure Iris wins. Isn't this the most exciting thing that's ever happened to you? It certainly is to me."

"Oh, yes," said Budge with her own smooth smile. There was nothing in the living room to indicate that anyone in the house was running for office.

I had thought that our mother's saying she had to go back to campaigning right off was only her overblown way of talking, but it turned out she meant this literally. As she gathered her things to leave, Polly asked me, "Maybe you'd like to go for a walk?" Another surprise: Polly was a year older than I, and it had always been Budge who was my friend.

Hugh said he was going to stay, and Budge took him upstairs to show him where he'd be sleeping, as if we'd never been in the house before. Polly said, "I'll tell Traudy," she and Budge came back wearing safari jackets, and we all ended up going out with "Tante" into the cool night air. Everything the two girls said to her on the way to the subway stop confirmed my impression that they were little automatons. I had never heard kids talk with such polish about nothing at all: "You must be happy to have Joan and Hugh back so soon." "Are you still happy at work?" "I'm so glad you got a chance to stop by." (Always a word like that: *happy, glad.*) The situation was even worse than I'd feared. Charles had turned them into cookie-cutter persons.

But once our mother was down the steps and out of sight, Polly took the rubber band off her ponytail and shook out her hair, which remained a little indented at shoulder level, and Budge said, "Iris won't let her wear it loose. She says it looks messy." I'd never heard a kid call a parent by his first name, and it made me rethink this social adroitness of theirs as perhaps not totally a bad thing.

Then Polly led us down the street, into an alley, and behind a boarded-up Greek restaurant, saying at the end, "All clear." She sat on her haunches between a rickety green topless Dumpster and a chain-link fence and took out of her jacket pocket a small hinged metal candy box from France. Inside were two very thin joints and several bits of crumpled tinfoil. After inhaling, she said, "You smoke?" in that little croaking way that showed she was trying to keep the air in her lungs.

Although I had only a few times, I nodded, pretending that this was an everyday occurrence for me, and, as we passed the joint, I thought about how there would always be certain compensations for the behavior required of rich kids. I had taken it for granted that they had nice vacations and lots of clothes. Now I could see they had more important stuff as well, like good marijuana. Already things were flashing on and off.

Budge and I had squatted beside Polly. Now I said, "Not a whole lot of room." I rose, kneading my legs, and finally I sat right down on the pavement, with my legs straight out in front of me.

"Sometimes we've had *ten* people back here," said Budge.

Polly, as the elder, got to correct her: "Maybe seven," she said. "And you weren't there that time."

"I was there when we had to climb the fence," said Budge. To me she said, "We had to climb the fence and run to the street on the other side of the lot."

Polly said, "I didn't think Terence was going to make it, but he did," and Budge said, "Terence must weigh two hundred pounds, don't you think?" and Polly said, "One seventy-five, anyway." I had a sudden vivid, irresistible picture of him and a few others slightly ahead of him scattering. The dark, velvety gray air—very different from the clear black night of the country—looked like it would be soft to run through.

"Polly has a hollowed-out book at school," said Budge. "Her room was searched once because someone said she was dealing, but they didn't find anything." Budge's tone was complicated: disapproving, but proud, even envious.

It was evidently a tone Polly was used to. "The book was about the Lipizzaners," she said to me. "I figured everybody would be past that stage by now, but no, all kinds of jerks asked to borrow it. I think I'll try the Bible next time." I was pleased by her consciousness of me as an audience. Back when we were kids, we'd all just been unreflectingly together.

"Polly offered Vi a joint once," said Budge.

"Vi? The Vi I met?" I asked.

"You met Budge's 'special friend'?" said Polly.

"She did say something like that," I said.

"Special as in Special Ed," said Polly. "You should have seen her face when I asked. She was shocked. But she was flattered, too. For a while there I thought she was going to tell Charles, but she never did. The best thing about Iris's running for office is that no one is home anymore. It was a great summer. The only time I'd see Charles was when he'd come out of his room in the morning, yelling, 'Where's my change? Where's my change?' " Here she started to laugh, so it got harder and harder to understand her. "He'd get me to help him look! It was too perfect! He always acts like he knows what's on your mind, when in fact he hasn't a clue, not one tiny clue." We were all giggling by then; it was impossible to stop.

"It's easy to forget Charles is a person," I said, "because he forgets it himself all the time."

"Isn't that the truth," said Polly, slapping the side of her knee.

Budge said, "He wears a shower cap sometimes. It's really dumb-looking."

After a while we stopped laughing so hard and Polly tried to say—very seriously—"Is it true that your father spent all his money buying his way out of nuthouses?" but she had broken down by the end.

"Jesus," I said, surprised. Then I recovered myself, laughed two little laughs that sounded like hiccups, and said, "Where did you get that?"

"We know *lots* of crazy people," said Budge. "The mother of a girl at school smeared her own shit on the walls. She has to have two people to take care of her at all times."

I said, "My father knocked a hole in the wall of the room with the piano." This was not quite true—all that resulted was a small dent—but the words seemed a sort of shorthand to explain his equally bizarre actual behavior, which was harder to encapsulate.

"Your mother's okay," said Polly.

"I guess," I said. "Yours is pretty cool."

"Yeah," said Polly, kind of trailing off.

There was so much to think about. I put my hands in my pockets as we fell silent. A plane, loud and low, was upon us, then gone. Around us were items of surprising textures and luminosities, and it took me a while to identify them as snack bags, empty cigarette packs, a solitary page or two from a newspaper. Each time I made an identification, I felt a great sense of discovery. Occasionally I would catch a little glitter or a trail of something out of the corner of my eye, but as soon as I'd turn my head it would be gone.

That night, when I shared Budge's room with her, she said, "Everyone at school knows about the Lipizzaner book. Polly likes it that people know. She's a terrible show-off. She curses out cops when she's with her friends. One of these days she's going to get into trouble she can't get out of. You watch."

Not ten minutes later, while Budge was off trying to wheedle something out of Traudy, our mother came in, sat down on the edge of the spread, and said, "It must be so great to see Polly and Budge after all this time. Can you believe how grown-up they are?"

"You're wrinkling the dust ruffle," I said.

"Oh, *no.*" She immediately redraped it and patted it smooth. "They keep their things so nicely, don't you think?" She sat down again. "Sometimes I think I'd like to be their age again, just so I could be their friend."

When we went for a walk the next morning, Polly and Budge were wearing Lilly Pulitzer dresses. Polly's had big tangerine-colored daisies, and Budge's had four panels of yellow, chartreuse, white, and hot pink. I was wearing my Indian print (the only dress I owned that still fit, actually), and we all leaned up against the fence instead of squatting. Polly had one knee up, which pulled open the side vents of the dress, but both she and Budge were being very careful. They hunched over each time they took a drag, afraid of falling ash.

I couldn't decide whether it was the dope that made the scene in the kitchen when we returned such an odd one. Vi McFall was sitting on a stool and talking on the phone, the long beige cord wrapped around her forearm, while Traudy stood in the middle of the room, watching her as if she were about to steal the silver. No one else was home.

Polly and Budge went through their usual "It's so nice to see you," "How is your husband?" and all that nonsense. Vi drank it all in. She said, "I couldn't resist telling you in person how good Iris's chances look right now. I suppose I shouldn't have come, but I think of you as my own daughters." She gave us all hugs, even me.

Traudy said, "Iris will rue the day."

"Whatever do you mean?" asked Vi, still somehow entangled with Budge. "I should think you'd be proud of her."

Traudy didn't answer right away, just looked at them balefully. Then she said, "She would be better off staying here." She closed her mouth tight at the end, as if she were holding lots back.

"I suppose in Liechtenstein a woman's place is in the home?" said Vi, humoring Traudy as she rocked Budge back and forth.

"Iris is very delicate," said Traudy, eyeing her with distaste. "It will be too much of a strain."

It was true that Iris had had a number of bizarre diseases—once she'd had a virus in her knee that had crippled her for a week—but I had never seen her look as unhealthy as Traudy did. Traudy was much younger than Iris, but she already looked a little wizened, with her turned-down nose and thin lips and thin eyebrows. She wore the same sweater every day from September to April and sometimes even later. Today the white cable-knit cardigan was buttoned at the neck and draped over her shoulders like a cape. When Hugh and I used to visit as kids, she would take an orange out of the refrigerator every night so it would be warm by morning. Otherwise, peeling the thick cold skin could turn her hands an icy greenish-white—the color of frostbite, she said.

"So, are you all ready to leaflet?" Vi asked us.

"Are you going to do it, too?" said Budge.

When Vi said she had to get back to headquarters, Budge let out that sort of pretend wail that can't help but sound sincere.

Traudy said, "I hope you don't plan on giving your mother any trouble."

"We never give anyone any trouble," said Polly with an injured air. She used to have terrible fights with Traudy, but generally she and Budge ignored the barbs in Traudy's remarks. I was thankful I had no similar person in my life, especially since our mother referred to her as "Iris's little treasure."

In the car, Vi said, "I can't imagine what I've done to make Traudy dislike me so."

Vi dropped Polly and me off in front of a supermarket. As soon as she was out of sight, Polly slipped the rubber band off her hair and onto her wrist. We had a fairly big bundle of leaflets, and for a while we passed them out in the hot sun. One woman said, "Oh, they're all the same," which Polly pretended not to hear, but mainly people just accepted the handouts in silence.

After about an hour Polly announced she was thirsty and swept into the supermarket. First off, she went to a checkout counter and asked where the sodas were. After we each had chosen one, she asked to speak to the manager, saying at the same time, "I'll carry that," and taking my soda from me. I hoped that meant she was going to pay for it.

The manager, who sat in a little wooden box opposite the automatic doors, was a round man with a great expanse of smooth flat chin below his mouth. When Polly asked if she could tape the leaflet to the window so that the bigger of the photos showed, he leaned back in his chair with a great creak. "My," he said. "You two look awfully young to be in politics."

"Not at all," I said, offended, but Polly gave him a big smile and said, in that fake voice she used for grown-ups, "Iris Eberlander is my mother."

"Well, well," he said. "If she's half as pretty as you, I want to see the picture." He held out his huge hand for it, and Polly had to shift both sodas against her chest in order to pass it to him.

"Yup," he said. "I can see a real family resemblance."

"Why, thank you," said Polly.

"So, what is she running for? Assembly*man*?" He chuckled. "I'll be sure to vote for her."

"She has very progressive views," I said.

He nodded complacently. "Good, good." Then he got a little nervous. "Not too progressive, I hope."

"I don't see how you can be too progressive," I said.

"Look, if there's a store policy about putting stuff up, I'll understand," said Polly.

"She doesn't advocate all sorts of nutty stuff, does she?" He was looking to Polly—*Polly*—for a reasoned reply.

"Of course not," she said.

"I should think you'd want to stand up and be counted," I said.

"It's just one itty-bitty picture," said Polly.

"All right, all right," he said. But then there was a whole to-do about the tape and where it should go; the operation seemed to take forever. On her way out, Polly gave leaflets to the cashiers, the customers, and a delivery boy who was poking a carton of eggs lengthwise into a half-full grocery bag. She was almost to the automatic doors when she went back and asked if there were any straws. There weren't, so Polly said, "That's all right. We'll make do somehow."

Outside she gave me my soda with an odd smile, so I said, "I guess I have to be a little less argumentative."

"It worked fine," she said. She gave a woman a leaflet.

I put my pile down on the sidewalk to make it easier to hold the can. I took a drink and said, "We forgot to pay for the sodas."

As soon as Polly rolled her eyes, I realized with a shock that that had been the whole point.

For lunch we had submarine sandwiches at an Italian restaurant. I was very hungry, and the food was delicious, but I had trouble eating it. I was the one who'd said I wanted lunch but had no money, and I'd said it, assuming that Polly would know how to walk out on the bill. She certainly had plenty of experience. In the restaurant she showed me a driver's license for a twenty-one-year-old "Bonnie Duff" and then put her hair up to demonstrate how she could pass for her. She told me that she never wasted money on anything that could fit into a pocket and that she'd once walked out of a store with a four-foot philodendron for her mother's birthday.

It struck me that rich kids had opportunities to be bad in more splendid ways than the rest of us did. Most people in my hometown knew who I was, for instance, and there were no large philodendrons for sale. The only real store was a little supermarket not too different from the one we'd been leafletting in front of. I tried to think of something as large you could walk out of there with—charcoal briquettes, maybe.

But mainly I thought about what I might have to do at the end of the meal. Run? I tried to picture this as subverting the system, but I wasn't too successful, and I didn't spend much time on the ethics of the situation. I just hoped that Polly realized I wouldn't know what to do.

I had given up on eating for a while when Polly said, "You done?" I looked at the cleanly scalloped edges of the bite marks on the roll and nodded mutely.

"You go ahead," she said, and I walked slowly out of the restaurant and into the street and down to the corner, all the while feeling like my left foot was dragging a little, my shoulders were too tense—really, nothing was working at all. But once I turned the corner, I sped up. Soon I broke into a run and didn't stop until I got to the supermarket, where I heard a thin, flat "Joan!" I did a great pantomime of looking around, but already I knew it was Traudy, and I knew she was in one of the cars on the curb. Yes, there she was, alone in Iris's Saab, with the windows rolled down. "I suppose you're not used to telling either of your parents where you're going," Traudy spit out, gripping the steering wheel as if it were about to struggle free. "They probably don't even notice. But I have certain responsibilities. I was supposed to pick up you and Miss Butter-in-Her-Mouth Polly and give you lunch."

At first I wanted to slap her across the face. Then I whirled around and ran back the way I'd come so she wouldn't see me cry. I ran down the street and turned right and ran down another street. I didn't see Polly. What did Traudy know, anyway? She knew nothing about the way I was brought up. She knew nothing about our parents. She was a ruling-class toady.

I wandered for a good long time, imagining various caustic and wounding responses I should have made. I didn't pay any attention to where I was going at first, but I eventually noticed a lot of signs in Arabic, so I figured I must be near our mother's apartment. Someday I wouldn't care what anyone said about our parents.

I kept circling here and there, not walking too slowly, so that I'd at least look like I knew where I was going. Then I spotted, far down the street, the pornographic movie theater that was around the corner from our mother's. I knocked on and buzzed at her door, but of course got no reply. For a while I sat in the well created by the descending steps, which meant that my shoulders and head were at street level. Anyone could have come along and kicked me in the face. I had kept my bundle of leaflets, so I read through one a couple of times. I wished I still had that submarine sandwich. I was ashamed that I hadn't been able to eat it.

My head started getting wavy with hunger as I peered straight out at the sidewalk, and I finally counted up all my change, figuring there was bound to be enough for something, even if it was only a roll. I found a Middle Eastern take-out place where I could afford the second-cheapest sandwich, with a little left over for tax or whatever. My usual terror of ordering an item I couldn't pay for had returned. It was a gyro, which I had never heard of, and the man sliced chunks off a huge spool of processed meat hanging from the ceiling. I brought it back to the well in the sidewalk. The meat was like a Slim Jim, with clearer spots that looked like canker sores.

The sun had fallen within reach of the buildings by the time I decided to go to Iris's election headquarters.

It wasn't long before I realized no one had missed me. Our mother spotted me walking in the door and said distractedly, "Where's Budge?"—even though she was right on the other side of the room, a white sash spelling out EBERLANDER draped over her shoulder. Our mother hurried off when I pointed her out among the crowd.

But I didn't care. I loved that storefront office immediately. It had a great functional smell, a mixture of old wood and fresh paint, and everything proclaimed its seriousness: the knee-high window ledges piled with lists and printouts, the charts and maps and posters all over the walls. How can I explain it? I loved the *size* of the place. It was as if something I knew well had started to pulse with a strange utilitarian glamour. The furniture could have come from my high school: dark-green metal desks with stainless-steel drawer pulls, cafeteria tables with mica tops supported by spatulate arrangements of folding iron legs, a large freestanding chalkboard to the right, facing out into the room. But on the desks and tables were at least a dozen phones, all being used, and on the chalkboard was a series of numbers I soon learned referred to election districts.

Years later, after I'd grown up and worked in various capacities at many different election-night events, I attended a dinner for a judge who was moving up to the federal bench. By chance I was seated next to an old Brooklyn pol. When I mentioned Iris, he said, "I'm surprised you took her path at all, considering. Though maybe you felt you had something to prove." The fellow had a reputation for bluntness, but, as usual, such split-second shrewdness missed its mark. Everything that happened after my initial step into Iris's headquarters did not matter so much as that first visceral impression, which seized me like a familiar pair of hands.

A tall, thin man came up beside me to take one of the plastic glasses of jug wine that sat amid some papers on a desk. "Do you think Iris is ready to lead the masses?" he said. He was dressed in a very fancy double-breasted suit, but he also had a big shaggy mane of gray hair, as startling atop his head as a Manx would have been. It took me a couple of minutes to recognize him as Iris's old friend Horace.

"Is she going to win?" I asked.

"She better. I have five hundred dollars invested in her, and I want to see some return." Horace's teasing manner worked fine with this remark, but was a bit grotesque with his next: "I thought it was a shame when your parents broke up. Your father and I had a real rapport." I couldn't tell if even he knew whether he was serious. He formed his words so carefully he seemed to talk with only the front part of his mouth.

It is hard for me now to remember how homogeneous everything looked back then. Grown-ups looked equal to me because they all looked the same. Very few, outside of the family, had the faintest of personalities. I did notice a few African-Americans (Negroes, as they were called then) over in a corner of the room, but I never spoke to them.

Early on, while I was standing by the wine with Horace and our mother, a man walked into the room, holding up his hand and saying, "Hi, Horace." This sounded like a greeting, but because his arm was straight out in front of him and his palm was at right angles to it, the effect was to check any movement that might have been made toward him.

"Joe," said Horace, lifting his glass.

"Isn't that Joe Zigo . . . ?" said our mother, her voice trailing off, as if she were mesmerized by the space the man had left behind.

"He's a local political commentator," Horace said to me.

"I'm always amazed by who Charles knows," said our mother.

I, on the other hand, thought that everyone in the room might as well be a Joe Zigo. But to me that was no different from assuming that everyone could afford nice sheets.

Soon Iris and Charles walked in, and applause rippled through the storefront. I hadn't seen them since the summer, but they looked the same. Iris was cool, white-faced, self-possessed; Charles was impatient and overbearing. Polly and Hugh were with them, as if they were the family, and several photographs were taken of the four of them as they walked in, which gave me the triple creeps. I didn't like Hugh smiling, either. It was so unlike him.

"We're going to win!" Iris shouted. Everyone turned to her with expectation, but she seemed surprised at how loud her voice had been, and she said nothing more to the room at large.

"I hope she doesn't wait too long to give her speech," said Horace. "Everyone's going to get tired and go home."

Charles shook hands with all the men, and Polly weaved her way toward me. To a woman wearing a leather necklace as complicated as a doily, Polly said, "I haven't seen you in ages."

To a man with a part down the center of his head, she said, "How is Mrs. Belley?"

To me, she said, "The candy store, near the church, in five minutes."

To a woman waving a finger, she said, "What's your son been up to lately?"

I was beginning to realize that Polly was opaque in a way that even Budge wasn't. When Polly weaved her way over to her, I could tell Budge was a little put out by the cursory message; her eyebrows were drawn together in what would have been a scowl on anyone else. But Polly kept weaving her way around the room and out the door, as smooth as reflected light.

Our mother said, "I feel like history is being made around me," and I snuck myself an abandoned glass of wine.

I was getting used to being outside in the dark with Polly. This time we hung back in the shadows created by the two display windows that jutted out on either side of the shop door. There wasn't much room, so we had to stand, and when I leaned against the glass and put my knee up in front of me, it was practically in Polly's lap. She said, "So you gave everyone the slip today." She used a mock admonishing grown-up voice that was remarkably similar to her regular grown-up voice. Then she said, "Pretty cool." She did not ask me where I'd gone. Instead she pulled yet another joint from her candy tin.

As we smoked, I said, "What happened at the restaurant?" and she said, "Nothing much. I waited 'til it got busy and then slipped out."

I was beginning to think of the detour in my afternoon as an adventure. Polly's distant treatment of my disappearance was a real kindness—or maybe something better, since she did not make me feel as if I were the object of kindness. That she relished the trickery as well was no surprise; since she hid everything good about herself right next to everything bad, you could no longer separate the two.

"Your brother doesn't do this," she said, holding up the joint, and I said, "No, he doesn't like it," and she said, "I guess if I had a brain like his I wouldn't mess it up, either."

I should have been annoyed, since this implied that messing up my brain was no great loss, but the world was getting soft, the air as thick as brocade.

Budge never showed up, so we headed back, walking slowly and happily through the night. It took me a while to recognize Charles. It was actually the shape of his head I picked out; I couldn't see much else. He was up near the storefront, about a half a block away. I could hear the happy buzz of volunteers through the door, and I could hear Polly's and my much sharper footsteps in the foreground. Polly slowed down even further, which was a little provoking. Soon I picked out the curve of Iris's hair; her head had shifted in front of a white IRIS EBERLANDER sign on a brick wall. As we came closer, I could pick out her dark coatdress, too. Charles was saying, "I haven't seen you all day." His tone embarrassed me. Petulant, playful, but almost whiny—it was like nothing I'd heard from him before. "I don't like it," he continued, and then I realized that Iris was not Iris, but Vi, and Charles was thundering at us: "Where have you been? Do you know that your mother has been looking all over for you?"

Polly's "handling" voice was unchanged. "I'm sorry you had to come look for us, Daddy," she said.

Inside, she said to me—fiercely—"Vi used to be his patient."

"Your father's?" I said, amazed, still blinking at the sudden bright yellow light.

"Yes," she said. Then she said to a man by a desk, "Dr. Ross, how good of you to come."

When I looked around the crowd, I couldn't believe I hadn't seen it before: There were two very different types of people present. There were the men, who were in easy-fitting turtlenecks and sport coats. And there were the women, whose hair was tightly bound and whose silk trousers fluttered nervously about their knees. The men, I figured, were psychoanalysts. The women all looked like patients.

I noticed our mother, then. She was on the other side of the room, with her head cocked and her hand on the sleeve of a man in a maroon vest. He was backed up against the wall, a faint smile on his lips; he could have been congratulating himself on her interest.

I was standing all alone, just a skinny little kid, when J. J. McFall caught sight of me and came over and told me how nice it was of me and Hugh to be there. He said, "Family is very important at a time like this," and I said, "The family as an institution is through."

He said, "What?" and I said, "The family is a joke, and it's gone on so long it's a pernicious joke." I said that no one took marriage seriously anymore. I mentioned day care, which I pictured as a small clean room where kids ate properly. I said, "I believe in Proudhon's idea of free-floating units of children and adults who will group and regroup as necessary. If we're lucky, this will happen in our lifetime."

J. J. took little nervous sips of wine as I spoke. When I was finished, he said, "You may find you feel differently when you're older."

I crossed my arms in front of me and said, "I very much doubt it."

At last Iris started to address the crowd: "You've all heard about how I got the district drinking fountains fixed. It may seem like a little thing, but changing little things is how you change big things. To be fair to everyone on a larger scale, you must be fair on a smaller scale. And isn't that why we're here? To make sure everyone has a fair shake? Young and old. Rich and poor. Everyone. Yes, even you, Shirley." This last was directed at a woman sitting on a desk and holding a manila folder in front of her face; everyone laughed.

Iris beckoned Polly to her then, and, when she couldn't pick out Budge, she beckoned me. I copied Polly's half turn, so that Iris could drape her arms on our shoulder blades. A crowd looks very different from the front than from the back; the faces were as focused and intent as faces in a mirror. Polly and I had been called up so that Iris could talk about "children," but I didn't mind. In fact, I was thrilled. As "children," Polly and I were things on a smaller scale, I think; also we were the future and some other stuff. I spent more time absorbing the light and heat from the faces than I did listening. I sensed that Iris was using Polly and me as shields, to deflect attention, criticism, even a specifically sexual scrutiny, but I didn't mind that, either. In a way it absolved me of my own excitement. I never doubted Iris. Of course she could do anything; she was an Eberlander, wasn't she?

1969

I was a sophomore that year. In the spring, I became friends with a girl named Ronnie, who'd been having an affair with our English teacher, a skinny, balding, mesmerizing man. I came into the picture after Ronnie's mother had found out and started supervising her afternoons as well as her evenings; every once in a while, the poor woman would knock on Ronnie's bedroom door and give us a plate of marshmallow treats or a fashion magazine "with an interesting article in it about how to wear jewelry." Her big, brittle smile was heartbreaking. Ronnie said that if she didn't have a friend over, the two of them would spend the time alternately screaming and falling into each other's arms, weeping. So far her stepfather had been kept in the dark. Ronnie lent me the teacher's copy of *Lolita,* making me smuggle it out under my slicker, and I was halfway through it before I realized that even Ronnie's lover must have thought of her as a child. To me, she was very sophisticated; my inexperience may have made me the perfect friend for her because I could so sincerely ridicule her mother's argument that she was too young to sleep with a thirty-four-year-old man. I mean, it wasn't Ronnie who was baking things out of Rice Krispies and reading articles on wearing jewelry.

Mainly we talked about our teacher, but Ronnie also liked to spin dilemmas that were almost ecclesiastical in flavor. (She was another ex-Catholic who'd stopped going to church when her parents divorced.) I discovered this interest early on, when, in return for her first confidences, I told her the story of Charles and Vi's embrace, my own sexual adventures being far too tame in comparison. Of course I hadn't actually seen Charles and Vi embrace, but this was no place for the ambiguity of the real event. My best friend, Leila, had soon forgotten the less fanciful version I told her.

Ronnie would muse, hugging a pink-and-white-striped pillow to her chest, "It's so hard to know what to do in such a case. Should you rat on one grown-up to another? Is it even considered ratting when grown-ups are involved? Your cousin obviously hasn't told anyone. And you say she didn't even act surprised. Assuming she at least knows, do you let on that you do, too?" I enjoyed these questions as much as she did, but the only aspect I ever applied to the real Charles and Vi was Ronnie's belief that Charles could lose his license. "It's just one of those taboos," she said. "Psychiatrists aren't allowed to sleep with their patients."

"Even if it was special teaching therapy?" I asked.

"That probably makes it worse, in the eyes of the law," said Ronnie, and in this I assumed she was an expert. The English teacher had apparently drawn the doctor/patient comparison to their own situation on a number of occasions. "It's a serious business," she said with some satisfaction. "And your cousin may have been unconsciously warning of that when she told you about their professional relationship."

Although Ronnie was the only student I knew who was sleeping with a teacher, this intersection between the spheres of kids and grown-ups seemed only slightly odder than most. Hugh and I and even our father lived very much in a world of kids. Most of the adults I got the chance to examine closely were on TV: people who found bodies or closed factories or spoke out (regressively) against sewers. Our father had no friends. He viewed others his age with hostility and suspicion, as if they were all trying to ferret out some horrible secret. He discouraged conversation with the mothers of his piano students, although they didn't really count, because they spent all their time with kids the way he did. When the mother of twin girls hung around after sitting through both lessons and said that a person could die in this town for lack of intelligent company, it sounded to me as if she was looking for a soulmate, but he replied frostily that leading composers and musicians had gone out of their way to ask him his opinions on various matters. She said she may not have met as many people as he had, but when she'd had to quit college, her history professor had told her it was a crime. The twins started going to a piano teacher in Albany.

The house got weirder and weirder. As far as I could tell, I was the only one who picked anything up, which basically meant that everything stayed where it dropped. Nothing broken was fixed; the tear in the screen lasted as long as I lived there—lasted, in fact, until Hugh came back from college one summer having learned how to repair it. Most disturbing to me was the number of things that disappeared. I never knew what would be gone. The first I noticed was the blender, which I used mainly to make myself chocolate milk shakes. A kid named Ted Post, who always wore short-sleeved white dress shirts, had just had his piano lesson, and I immediately assumed that he'd taken it for some sick purpose of his own. I marched into the room where the piano was and started to yell without taking a good look at our father—always a mistake. "Where's my blender?" I screamed. "I can't believe the losers you teach. You call up Ted Post right now and tell him to bring back my blender."

"That blender was your mother's, and I sent it back to her," said our father in a thin, steely voice that was scarier than any yelling. So I never again mentioned the disappearance of any small appliance, except once, when it was the mixer, and it was the week of Hugh's birthday. That day I ended up throwing a glass of water at our father and locking myself in my room until he went for one of his drives. When the kitchen was close to empty, the pictures started disappearing off the walls. They were nothing much—framed prints no one looked at anymore. The all-green Cezanne landscape in the living room was the first to go. The house got barer and barer, but never airier or more spacious, the way a room does when you've taken up the carpet. The outlines left by the missing pictures were like stopped-up windows.

Whenever our mother called, our father would stalk up and down, swinging something in his hand, and then eventually hiss that he, too, was going to take off because he was tired of playing nursemaid. And all the while our mother would be telling us that everyone at school loved Budge and that when a student was supposed to show a few trustees around, she was the one chosen to do it, even though she was only in her second year. Or that one of Polly's teachers had designated her "the student showing the most improvement." She was always so cheerful! She and Budge charmed parents and pupils alike by singing a few verses of "Snoopy's Christmas" at the school's annual Christmas party. "Huh," I would say, and "How interesting." Not that Hugh and I got less discouraging when our father stormed out to drive around the back roads. The freezing responses would continue: "Is that so," and "That must have been nice."

Actually, most of our mother's references to the Eberlanders were to the grown-ups. Their brownstone seemed to be a place where adults were the norm rather than the exception, and this may have been another reason I told Ronnie about Charles and Vi, despite my resentment at having the Eberlanders constantly thrust upon me: Ronnie had her glimpse into the adult world; I had mine.

And what a glimpse! I was just as monosyllabic when our mother told me that Iris stayed at one of the finest hotels when the Assembly was in session, that her name had already been in the *Times* twice, and that the Speaker had heard of Charles Eberlander. But, in truth, I harbored an unquenchably romantic notion of Iris. Hers was not the way I imagined going into politics myself. Officeholder, appointee—the words had no color. If I pictured making money at all, it was as the owner of a small shop where people would lean across the counter and talk—argue at first, but then eventually come 'round and start to attend meetings after hours, when the real world-transforming work would be done. The room I could picture better than the discussions or the plans. It would be small and dim—utilitarian, but in a cluttered, late-Victorian, early-Marxist sort of way. I expected this kind of comfort, too: I always imagined I would have a very nice umbrella, for instance.

But if Iris was a politician instead of a revolutionary, she was as close as I'd ever come across in this extremely flawed country. This, combined with her powdered face, her dramatic medical history, her exhilarating posture—why, I even thought of her with a little ache sometimes, the way I thought of someone holding me.

So by the time the next July Fourth weekend rolled around, I was perfectly willing to accompany Hugh to New York for the Atlantic Open. And I hardly minded when our mother greeted us by crying, "Budge is home this year! Can you believe it?" Our mother looked much the same as she had the year before, except she was wearing a tie-dyed T-shirt dress in shades of red and rose and maroon that made her sandy hair look a little too reddish itself. Also, she was wearing silver peace-sign earrings and lots of skinny silver bangle bracelets. "I can't wait," she said. "I haven't seen any of the Eberlanders in weeks."

While we were waiting for the subway, she said, "Budge called Aaron the 'Big Dandelion' the other day, which is pretty funny, because that's exactly what he looks like."

"Who's Aaron?" I asked, and then immediately wished I hadn't; our mother was so clearly happy to say, "He's a man I've been seeing."

I'd thought Hugh wasn't listening, but here he started to laugh.

"The gray, fuzzy kind of dandelion," said our mother, as if that were somehow better. "Not that he's gray, heaven forbid. He's blond. But his hair is soft and curly and sticks up in all directions. Budge said she's never seen hair like it."

"Oh, really," I said.

"And Iris said she had a good time talking to him the other day."

"Isn't that nice," I said.

"Don't worry—you'll get to meet him," she said. "He can't believe I didn't show you the sights last year."

The subway was as hot as the year before. The Eberlanders' street was as pretty. The Eberlanders' house was as austere. But the person who opened the door was Vi. "Oh!" she said. "We weren't expecting you until later." She was wearing wide-legged blue trousers that I don't think Iris would have worn, but otherwise she still looked like an echo, with her pulled-back hair and her powdered face and her pearl earrings.

"I don't think we had any special luck with the trains," said our mother. We were all standing in the foyer.

"Budge won't be back for another hour," said Vi, looking at me, and our mother said, "Where's Iris?"

"The office," said Vi. Then her face changed, and her nice laugh crackled out. "Do I sound like the abandoned housewife?"

We were all still standing just a couple of feet inside the door, stuck near the grandfather clock. It occurred to me that we might never move, because our mother didn't feel it was her place to walk in without being invited, Vi didn't feel it was her place to do the inviting, and, as far as I could tell, she was all alone in the house. So I said, "I have to use the bathroom."

"So do I," said Hugh, and everybody sort of broke apart.

"You know where they are?" said Vi, and laughed again. "Of course you do."

I used the one on the first floor and stayed longer than I had to. I ostentatiously looked at myself in the mirror over the tiny pedestal sink, a mirror whose silver frame was twisted into leaves and snakes. Then I just as ostentatiously looked in the direction of the lace-curtained window. Sometimes my face looked so familiar and normal to me, it was a surprise.

When I finally left the room, Vi was waiting for me on a stool in the kitchen. Perhaps I'd sensed her presence, and that was why I'd lingered. "Have you talked to Budge lately?" she called out. That long, sharp nose of hers on her round, flat face had the look of a pin stuck in a pin cushion.

"Not since last year," I said, hovering around the door.

"You know I feel very close to Budge," she said.

I nodded, coming closer.

"I worry about her. It's so difficult, growing up without a mother. But why should I be telling you that? You know better than anyone."

"Budge has a mother," I said.

"Budge has a *great* mother," she corrected me. "If she weren't so great, it wouldn't matter that she was never around."

"Budge is okay," I said.

Vi nodded. "I know," she said. "Of course I like to think I fill in the gaps a little. That's why I hang around here." She seemed to be watching me to see how I would take this.

"Don't you work, too?" I asked.

The question flattered her. "I don't exactly have a full schedule," she said. "J.J. wouldn't have liked it, because I have to do so much entertaining for him. And I never pushed hard enough for referrals, so I have a lot of free time. I like to think that if you add me to Iris, you might come up with one full-time mother. Not that I could ever take Iris's place, you understand. But sometimes it's better to talk to someone who's not a parent, don't you think?"

"On communes the kids treat all the adults as parents," I said.

"Ah," said Vi. "I can tell that you see exactly what I mean."

But I backed off. "It's just something I read about," I said.

Vi went on as if I hadn't spoken: "The work Iris is doing is very important. I'm probably not supposed to say it, but I don't think Charles appreciates that fact. Your mother does, I know, but Charles is a little cynical about politics, and he puts a bit too much faith in the use of force, the way all men do. Not that what Charles does isn't important, too. That goes without saying. It's such a privilege to know your aunt and uncle; I don't know why I should have been so lucky. They're both so . . . so good. I'm convinced that there are people alive today solely because of Charles's treatment. He's a brilliant, brilliant man. He has a way of reaching out and seizing the heart of something. And it's not only the people who have been in analysis with him who've benefited. He's opened the minds of a whole generation of psychoanalysts. He is an inspiration."

She looked up at me in an expectant, vulnerable sort of way, and I was struck by how much younger she was than Charles, or even Iris. Her ponytail made her look like a surfer's girlfriend.

I heard Charles at the door then, and Vi said in a low voice, as if we'd been exchanging confidences, "We'll have to continue this another time."

We could hear our mother from the next room: "Charles! I haven't seen you in ages! Where did you get that tan? I don't think I've ever seen you with a tan before."

But Charles couldn't have exchanged more than a few lines with her before he was in the kitchen, clasping my hand with a fervor I had never seen before. He shook my hand firmly, as if I were a colleague. "You remember Iris's best friend, Vi," he said, indicating her perch on the stool with a turn of his body. In anyone else I might have assumed this was friendliness, but in Charles it was a sign of uneasiness: He was not quite so sure of everything as he wanted to appear.

"Joan and I have been catching up," said Vi, giving me a complicitous smile.

"Great, great," he said, clapping his hands together. "Vi helps out a lot when Iris isn't around. Budge is so fond of her, you know."

"Where is Budge?" I asked.

"Isn't she supposed to be here?" Charles asked Vi.

This laugh of Vi's was a little like cellophane uncrumpling. "I am not her jailer," she said.

We talked for a while longer in the kitchen—Charles, Vi, our mother, and me. Charles loosened his tie as if he always did, when in fact I had never seen him do it before. The room wasn't as warm as it had been, or maybe this was just an illusion caused by the sun's descent in the sky. The blue-flowered ceramic tile looked cool to the touch. Early on I almost asked about J.J. and then I thought maybe I wouldn't. It wasn't long, however, before our mother went right ahead. Vi said that J.J. was fine. "Of course he works very hard," she said. "I hardly ever get to see him anymore."

"That's a shame," said our mother. "He has such a good heart."

"I know," said Vi. "I know better than anyone."

"Do you know what we're having for dinner?" said Charles.

"Gazpacho," said Vi. "It's in the refrigerator."

"You remember how good Vi's gazpacho is," said Charles to our mother.

"Oh?" she said, looking from one face to the other. "I'm sure it is."

Then Budge came in, switching on lights. We heard her drop something on a chair. Appearing in the doorway, she said,

"What's up, mate?" in a fake English accent that made me think she was high. She grinned, and I briefly wished I'd somehow smoked one of the two joints I'd brought from home.

"Where have you been?" said Charles. He used a tone of voice that would have left me for dead.

"I'm very sorry," said Budge, apparently unconcerned. "But I told you I was going to be with Odette, and you know how she is. She was having another *crise.*" She hugged me and Vi and "Tante." Up close, she smelled of marijuana, but she was dressed in a very saucy, girl-next-door fashion: gleaming white shorts and sneakers, pink top with little white daisies on it.

"She was having a crisis in a place without phones?" said Charles, but clearly he was mollified.

"I wish I'd had a friend like you when I was your age," said our mother.

"Gadzooks, me pretty," said Budge, leaving me in no doubt about her state of mind.

I suggested that the two of us go upstairs.

At dinner, Charles said, "What's with your friend Odette, anyway? She always looks so scruffy."

"It's her job," said Budge.

"What does that mean?" said Charles sharply.

Budge was turning on the charm. "Her mother takes one look at her and gives her twenty-five dollars to go to the hairdresser. So Odette gets a friend of hers to cut her hair, and she's twenty-five dollars richer. The only drawback is that her hair doesn't look super great. It's amazing that people can behave that way, isn't it?"

"And I suppose you think the parents are completely in the dark about this," said Charles. "Well, let me tell you that parents understand a great deal more than you imagine. It's not so easy to fool them as it might appear."

"Oh, Budge," said Vi, who was sitting in Iris's chair. "You don't cut her hair, do you?"

"Are you kidding?" said Budge. "You can't do anything like that around here. No one ever tries to fool Charles." This was a leap that would have baffled me if Budge had not told me upstairs that Odette had originally gotten her idea from Polly and that it was Polly who had first referred to the practice as her "job." When I'd objected that Polly's hair looked fine, Budge said that I hadn't seen it lately.

Budge also told me that she was supposed to have been at a tennis camp in Pennsylvania, but her father had changed his mind at the last minute, saying she was too young. "He's demented," she said. "How could I have been old enough to go last year and not this year? Maybe I got younger as time passed." She didn't seem to mind about the camp, which she hadn't liked much, but she had nothing to do instead. "We hardly ever get to go up to Cold Spring," she said. "Iris doesn't have the time."

Her resentment didn't show at dinner, however. It looked as if she really did like Vi. You could almost say that Budge was having fun. She giggled quite a lot. I was surprised to see how informal the meal was; I guess I'd always assumed that Charles was responsible for the usual stiffness. But here he was looking downright benign as Budge kept popping up and down to get things to show us. She'd saved a postcard of a nineteenth-century Russian chess set for Hugh and only laughed when he said, "You couldn't really use a set like that. It would be too distracting."

Her good humor wasn't catching, though. Our mother talked less than usual, and Traudy, who had come up from her basement apartment at the last moment, was very gloomy and said almost nothing at all.

Vi fetched things from the kitchen several times, leaving her discarded napkin standing up by her plate like a knee under a sheet. In between these trips, she talked about how great Iris was. She said that Iris was the only person she knew who might have a real effect on the world.

Charles said, "It sounds like Odette's got a cure for the unemployment problem." His uncharacteristically playful manner made me so nervous that even I found it hard not to laugh.

I said, "The only answer to the unemployment problem is a complete restructuring of the economy."

Traudy said, "Whose table are you sitting at, little miss?" but it turned out she was talking to Budge, who had twisted sideways in her chair—evidently a proscribed position.

Charles said, "It always surprises me that people like Odette try these deceptions, when there are no such things as secrets."

"Is that some sort of riddle?" asked our mother, and Vi said, "What Charles means is that anything anyone tries to hide manifests itself in one way or another."

"You mean it screws them up?" I asked.

"That's one way," said Vi.

"Odette's already so neurotic, no one would notice," said Budge cheerfully.

After dinner Charles and Vi took snifters of brandy into the living room, where Budge sat on the footstool of Vi's chair. I got the impression that she preferred to be there rather than with me, so when our mother insisted on helping Traudy with the dishes, I helped, too—or at least I hung around the kitchen for a while. The two of them were pretty quiet until Traudy suddenly said, "I am not used to American ways," with what struck me as a dangerous air of simplicity.

"But, Traudy, you fit in so well," cried our mother. "I would never do so well in a foreign country. You've become one of the family."

Whose family? I thought.

"There are some things I do not understand," said Traudy, pursing her lips in a fake attempt at comprehension. "Is it usual for a woman's best friend to take her place at the table when she's away?"

"Oh, don't worry about that," said our mother. "Americans are not so rigid about where everybody sits."

Iris still had not come home by the time Vi left.

It was Aaron Lemon who took Hugh to the McAlpin the next day. Since the Fourth wasn't until Friday, our mother didn't have Thursday off as she had the year before. She was sorry she was going to miss a day of our company. She was also sorry she wasn't going to have a chance to introduce Aaron to us herself. But she figured we wouldn't want to get up as early as she had to, especially since the tournament didn't start until after noon. So instead she told us a great deal about this Aaron fellow: He had the same car as Vi, he grew up in New Jersey only twenty-five miles from J.J., someone Polly knew was thinking of going to the same two-year college he had attended, Iris had talked about Albany with him, and soon after he met Charles they ran into each other at a magazine stand near Radio City Music Hall. "Isn't that the funniest coincidence?" asked our mother. "Charles didn't recognize him at first. But they haven't had much of a chance to get to know each other. I'd love to ask Aaron out to the country house sometime, but I'm afraid to suggest it. Charles is so straight-laced, and of course we're not married."

Hugh and I were all ready to go when the buzzer sounded, but Hugh immediately took out his magnetic chess set and started to whip around the pieces. While he stayed in the kitchen, I went with Traudy to the door. I'd been given a choice: I could accompany Budge to her (local) tennis lesson with the hope that Traudy could get me into it, too—in which case I might be able to use an old racquet of Polly's, if it could be found—or I could see the sights with Aaron. So I was stuck with him. And when Traudy, with her sweater draped over her shoulders as usual, slid off the chain, withdrew the bolt, and turned the knob, there he was, with his head cocked and his thumbs hooked in his dirty white jeans, as if to say, "Hey! Look at me!" His hair was whitish blond and very curly, standing three inches from his scalp in all directions. He was short and thick through the chest and waist and thighs. He was wearing granny glasses and a blue work shirt like the one I had decided against putting on. I wasn't great at gauging grown-ups' ages, but I knew people in town like him: He couldn't have been more than thirty years old. He said, "Hi, guys."

Traudy clutched the bottom corners of her sweater with crossed hands and said, as if confirming her worst fears, "Are you Aaron Lemon?"

"Yeah," he said, and sauntered in. A red bandanna trailed out of his back pocket.

He actually reminded me of two different guys back in our hometown, both of whom still hung out with high school students, one because he was a contractor who hired a lot of them part-time, and the other because he was often hired along with them. I had just met these two this past year. (They were not the sort Hugh had anything to do with.) They looked overgrown to me, and a little sickly. They had their own apartments, where they smoked a lot of dope, but they were always wandering through their parents' houses, looking for some kind of special saw or a book on UFOs or something. I found their pale-faced cockiness odd. I mean, at their age, who did they have to be cocky *toward*?

To me Aaron said, "Don't take this the wrong way, but you look like a Joan." Then he said, "Where's the prodigy?" He paused to peer into the living room, and I think Traudy was afraid he was going to go in, but he headed on back to the kitchen, bandanna bouncing. Hugh pointedly did not look up until Aaron was right beside him, saying, "Pawn to queen's bishop five."

Then Hugh looked up and appeared to contemplate him for a moment. "You're allowing your queen and your rook to be forked," he said.

"Oh, yeah?" said Aaron. "Let's see." Hugh played out a few moves, palming two of the pieces, and Aaron said, "You didn't have to exchange."

"Yes, I did," said Hugh, returning all of the pieces to their original positions. He didn't bother to elaborate.

"Okay, you win," said Aaron. "Let's go. I hope you roast them all. Just don't be afraid to come out on top. Someone's got to be on the bottom, but it doesn't have to be you. That's my motto."

I was again wearing my Indian-print dress, whose repeated-moon pattern echoed the mirrors on the tangerine-colored purse I carried. My two joints were in a slit in the purse's padding, which gave me a certain confidence. I said finally, "What is a Joan supposed to look like?"

"I knew you'd take it the wrong way," said Aaron.

Traudy said, "Joan, maybe you'd like to stay and wait for Budge. She won't be long," and I said, "No, no."

"We're going to have *fun,*" said Aaron. Looking at me full in the face for the first time, he added, "I can show you places your mother's never dreamed of." I made a point of meeting his gaze; anything less would have been cowardly. Traudy, on the other hand, refused to look at me as we took off.

On the way to the subway, Aaron asked me, "How do you like the city? Pretty different from East Podunk or wherever it is you're from, isn't it?"

"It's different," I said.

Then Aaron said to Hugh, "How do you like it?" and Hugh said, "What?" and Aaron said, "How do you like the city?" and this time Hugh didn't bother to answer at all. At the McAlpin he insisted we leave him in the lobby. Aaron tried to argue with him, but Hugh had a way about him that suggested he, personally, didn't care what the outcome of a discussion was, but he knew what it was going to be, anyway. In the end Aaron said, "He doesn't like me much, does he?"

I shrugged.

"It makes sense," said Aaron. "I'm moving in on his territory." He bought the *Voice* at the magazine stand, while I stood next to a couple of men in dark suits speaking Russian and smoking cigarettes. Every time they took a drag, they tried to flick their ashes into a big brass bird bath–shaped ashtray. As far as I could tell, no ash ever got a chance to accumulate. After Aaron had pocketed his change, he said something like "pree-vette" to them.

They at first looked at him blankly; then one said tentatively, "Yes? Hello?"

Aaron nodded to them benignly. "How ya doin'?" he said. On our way out he said, "I'm half Russian, you know."

It made me feel very grown-up to walk down the street with Aaron. Everyone seemed to recognize my right to be with him, because no one gave us a second glance. I swung my bag a little, letting it knock rhythmically against my thigh. Aaron had a bouncy, bad-boy sort of step. "I thought we'd see the Empire State Building first," he said, and I said, "Oh, good," as if I'd been thinking exactly the same thing.

Thirty-fourth Street was crowded, full of men in light jackets and women in short, bright-colored dresses. Aaron said they were all on their lunch hour. "Pathetic, isn't it?" he said. "Punching the clock like that, I mean."

I asked him why he didn't have to be at work.

"I am temporarily between engagements," said Aaron. "Besides which, I'm really a drummer. Didn't your mother tell you that?"

Another musician, I thought, but then I thought—naah, he's not a musician.

"We used to play at Nolan's Saturday night," he said, changing my mind not one fraction.

"Hunh," I said.

"We played top-forty stuff, mainly. That's what people want to hear. And it's a lot harder than you might think." He was walking quite fast—on purpose, it seemed to me—and it was a little hard to keep up with him, so I stopped suddenly and stared at some clothes in a store window. There was a long yellow culottes-like pants suit, with a high waist and tentlike double folds in the leg. There was a sleeveless double-breasted navy dress with a short flaring skirt and big gold chains at the waist. There was a suit of diagonal pink-and-green plaid with alternating pink and green buttons down the front. Aaron must have walked ten yards before he realized I wasn't beside him. When he came back, he said, "You girls are all alike. What's the point in looking?" which annoyed me to no end. Then he added, "Oh, don't look so glum. I'll buy you anything your little heart desires when I make my first million."

Later on down the block, he said, "I guess the Eberlanders can afford anything their hearts desire right now, can't they?" and I finally said, "I wouldn't know."

"A house like that," he said. "I'm sure they could. And that weird nurse with a sweater on in the middle of the summer! It must be eighty degrees out. Wow. Help me to the funny farm, that's all I can say. How do you stand it?"

"They have a country house, too," I said.

He laughed. "You like them for their country house?" he said. "Now that's something I can understand."

Actually, I had been responding to his earlier assessment of the Eberlander wealth—pointing out that it should be adjusted higher—so I said, "No," in some confusion, and he said with glee, "Now she's taking it back!"

There was no way to win with someone like him.

The higher you went in the Empire State Building, the seedier it got. The lobby was several stories high; the dark marble was splashed with plum- and chocolate-colored veins; there were scallops in the walls and bronze-edged lozenges in the floor. The first elevator you got into was just a bland box, though, and you waited for the next one halfway up in a little dingy hall. The walls of this second elevator were scratched, the plastic that covered the light in the ceiling was broken, and blackened chewing gum was ground into the E.S. on the floor.

The observation tower was mainly windows, but I saw right off that New York was not at its best when seen from this height. It became in its own way ordinary—and colorless. When I was on the street, there was a constant roiling of faces and clothes and cars and signs and lights and shops and sawhorses and street vendors. I still couldn't get used to it. But from eighty-five stories up, even in the bright sun, everything was gray. The browns were gray, the tans were gray, the greens were gray, the reds were gray.

The view was something different. I felt it as soon as we went out onto the balcony and Aaron said, "Whoa, there," grabbing my bare upper arm, even though there were so many guy wires crisscrossed above the observation deck he obviously wasn't worried that I was about to dive overboard. It was a heady feeling—not a feeling of power, as you'd think, but a feeling of insignificance, a feeling of dizzying, liberating, expectant insignificance. There was no wind.

Aaron put his hand on my upper arm again to guide me past an enviable couple speaking French and two older ladies wearing Polaroid sunglasses. He put his hand on my arm to position me in front of the binoculars. He put it there when he was pointing out the East River and the United Nations. He put it there to exclaim, "Look at that boat!" He put it there to turn me around. I noticed a few other young people. Most had long hair and jeans, but there were three guys in crew cuts wearing dress whites. I couldn't imagine what made anyone join the military in this day and age.

In the elevator going down, I said, "When are we going to have lunch, anyway?" and Aaron said, "As soon as we get to the restaurant." He laughed a little, and his eyes darted around as he said this; you could tell he was very aware of the other people in the car. He was first off the elevator, red bandanna bobbing. I liked his work boots, at least, with their cord laces and their thick, thick wrinkles.

He showed his first uncertainty outside the restaurant, reading the menu and saying, "It looks very English, doesn't it? Very Ye Olde English Pub." He said this with a pseudo-British accent that reminded me of Budge. Instantly I decided he couldn't afford the place—an idea I just as instantly decided to ignore.

"Aren't we going in?" I said.

The restaurant had a brick front, with a many-paned window, a fanciful brick window ledge, and two iron street lamps flanking the door. I now doubted he'd ever been inside, but it had been his choice, after all.

"Well?" I said.

"Royalty first," he said, bowing low and gesturing me through the door.

It was very cold inside. We did not exactly fit in with the lunch crowd, and I was already getting goose bumps, but the waitress didn't think it strange when Aaron said we wanted a table for two. I felt some regret when she gave us our oversize menus and he said, "I paid ten dollars for a beer at the Sherry Netherland." But she didn't appear to hear, and he was forced to address his next remark to me. "Yep, I was waiting for a friend. Expense account—*you* know."

I ordered a small steak, only because I figured I'd never finish a big one, and he ordered a hamburger and a beer.

"I guess you've caught pretty expensive tastes from being around the Eberlanders," he said. "Thank God your mother hasn't. I'd be broke."

I thought about this. Then I said, "But you don't pay for her, do you?"

"I have to pay for myself, don't I?" he said. "No one buys Aaron Lemon. No one."

"Well, I don't think that's what she has in mind," I said.

"Oh?" he said. He went on suggestively, "And what do you think she has in mind?"

I just looked at him.

He said, "The other day I noticed she had a new pocketbook, so I mentioned it to her, and she goes, 'That's not new. That's just my summer purse.' She has one purse for the summer, one for the winter. Isn't that wild?"

I shrugged, looking away now.

"Do *you* have one purse for the summer and one for the winter?"

"Of course not," I said scornfully.

"She's one wild woman," he said, shaking his head.

I couldn't tell whether he was being sarcastic; it seemed to me that having two purses was the very opposite of being wild, so I sensed a trap. This feeling was heightened by the close way Aaron was watching me. "What with Charles Eberlander being your uncle and all, I suppose you know what purses stand for," he said.

Fortunately the food arrived then, and although I didn't finish it all, I ordered pecan pie and coffee for dessert, while Aaron drank another beer. "Hey, I might as well live it up," he said. "Maybe I can send your mother a bill."

Outside in the bright, hot, glaring sunlight, Aaron reached for me again, but this time his hand went past my nearer arm to my far shoulder—his grip was in fact fierce—and he kissed me hard on the mouth, so hard that I could feel the ridges between his teeth. As soon as he did, I realized I had known he would from the moment I first saw him at the Eberlanders' door. "You're pretty hot stuff, aren't you?" he said, and since this was my secret assessment of myself, I did not demur. I kissed him back. I hooked my thumb in the pocket with the bandanna. "My God," he said. "I knew it! I knew it!"

We began to walk again, back the way we'd originally come, which was still crowded with people. We held hands for a moment, but they got too sweaty. "It wouldn't take long to get to my place," said Aaron. "And I've got about a half an ounce of grass, some of the best you'll ever try."

It occurred to me that Aaron was someone I could learn something from. So I said, "Okay." Then, in the hot swollen air of the subway, I started having second thoughts. I said, "Do you have air-conditioning?"

"I've got a fan," he said. "I always watch TV naked in front of the fan."

"I see," I said. Second thoughts or no, I was no longer afraid of these remarks of his.

Aaron's building was a big brick box near Fourteenth Street, about a dozen windows across and a dozen windows tall, most of which had some kind of display: a torn curtain, wind chimes, plants, shells, glass bottles, a cat. Real hippies were sitting on a broken-down sofa in the lobby. At least, they both had hair down their back, and headbands, and they both said, "Far out," to us as we headed up the stairs. I had never been in such a fabulous place. When we got to Aaron's floor, however, you could hear the TV down the hall, and inside his apartment was a guy around Aaron's age—skinny, gray-faced, wearing a withered dress shirt, sleeves rolled to the elbow. Aaron slammed the door and said, "What are *you* doing here?" but it soon became clear that this fellow was his roommate and had even made the down payment on the leather recliner he was ensconced in. Aaron did not bother to introduce me. When the roommate lowered the volume on the TV, the man asking questions on the screen looked awfully familiar, but it wasn't until after he put up his hand in a gesture of benediction that I cried, "That's Joe Zigo!"

"Got it in one," said the roommate.

"I saw him at Iris's election headquarters," I said. "Iris Eberlander, that is. She's my aunt."

Aaron and the roommate exchanged glances. The room was nearly empty, holding only the recliner, the TV, an olive-green carpet remnant, and a yellowish couch.

"Who's that he's interviewing?" I asked.

"Who knows?" said the roommate.

"Don't you have someplace to go?" Aaron asked the roommate.

"He's some Democrat spouting off about something," the roommate said to me.

"Oh," I said, catching his tone of disapproval. "What are you, some sort of Socialist?"

"I'm a Republican," he said.

I sat down on the couch, dumbfounded. I turned to Aaron, who was still sulking by the door, and said, "How about you?"

"How about me, what?" said Aaron crossly.

"Are you a Republican?"

"I'm not anything," he said. "But I don't see that it matters. And don't talk to me about stuff you don't know anything about."

"What about Lindsay?" said the roommate.

"Still," I said. "It's unbelievable." I had never met a Republican who dressed the way they did. Even Charles wasn't a Republican.

The argument sputtered out, but there were a lot of bad feelings. Aaron soon said, "Come on. I've got to get you back to your mother." He didn't touch me again.

At the McAlpin our mother asked me if I'd had a good time, and I said I had.

"I knew you would," she said happily, and Aaron, who was still in a sour mood, said, "She sure has a lot of opinions. You wouldn't think so at first."

"I knew you two would get along," said our mother. "What a perfect day! Iris is going to make us dinner . . . Just the family, I mean."

"Hey, don't mind me," said Aaron. "I'm only the babysitter."

This time when we knocked on the Eberlanders' door, it was Iris who answered. She was wearing an apron with a rose appliquéd on the pocket; she never wore irises. Budge was there, too, saying in her clear, piping voice, "Come in, come in," and "Did you have a nice time?" and (to me as well as to our mother) "What can I get you to drink?"

I was just standing there smiling. I hadn't realized how shy I was going to feel around Iris. All I could think of was other stuff our mother had told me: Iris had a little traveling steam iron, which was a wonder; our mother had tried it, even though she didn't believe in owning clothes that needed ironing. Iris could get from New York to Albany and back on just a little more than one tank of gas. Iris had gotten a mash note from a page. Iris was thinking of having her own phone line put in.

"I hope you like shrimp," said Iris, displaying her open palms.

"Shrimp!" cried our mother. "My God, shrimp! Well, I ought to be able to choke down a couple."

Iris had put her hands up on either side of her face. "Kiss these two for me, will you, Budge? I'm all shrimpy." I couldn't remember ever kissing her and so took this as an invitation: I pecked Iris's beauty mark. Her hair was less elaborately coiffed than it had been—the French twist had turned into a French bun—but it was just as severe, and other than that, she looked pretty much the same.

"Isn't Hugh coming?" said Budge. I couldn't tell how real the disappointment in her voice was.

"Hugh is still at the McAlpin," I said.

Our mother said, "I thought it might be different this year, and they might start earlier."

"Why would it be different?" I asked, and she shrugged.

"Just walking into this house makes me happy!" she exclaimed, heading down the hall, looking into rooms. "And where's Charles?" she asked. When Iris said he was at the office, our mother went on, "So we're just the ladies now, eh?" She sat down on one of the stools in the kitchen as Iris went back to deveining the shrimp. "I always had more men friends than women friends," said our mother. "I don't know why."

"Maybe you like being with men better," said Iris, wiping her forehead with the back of her wrist.

"But it's nice to have a friend like Vi, isn't it?" asked our mother. "I mean someone you can really count on."

Iris agreed that this was so.

"The truth is, you're my Vi," cried our mother. "I don't know what I'd do without you."

Iris was embarrassed. "I certainly hope you don't get a chance to find out," she said.

I was helping Budge cut up tomatoes for a tomato salad. We weren't talking to each other, so I suppose we were listening in. Anyway, our mother lowered her voice for the next remark: "Is it true that Charles has become you-know-who's psychiatrist?"

At first I thought she was talking about Vi, but then I realized she couldn't be: That had been over long ago.

"You-know-who?" echoed Iris.

Our mother looked pointedly at me and Budge. "The one who's been in the papers," she said.

"I don't know who you mean," said Iris.

"It's all right," said our mother. "My lips are sealed."

Iris said, "Budge, will you bring me the big blue bowl?" as our mother mused, "Imagine carrying around the secrets of all those important people. What an awful burden."

Charles came home then in what was a remarkably close replay of the evening before. Our mother greeted him at the door, but he was once again in the kitchen almost immediately, loosening his tie. This time he was content to nod at me, but still I sensed his initial uneasiness. He was checking things out: Was Iris as he'd left her? Was Budge? Was the counter? The stools? The blue-flowered tile? He didn't kiss Iris to greet her, but I'd never known him to do that.

The tablecloth, cutlery, plates, glasses, and serving dishes were basically the same as the night before, except more elaborate, as befitted a celebration of sorts. Hugh was missing, but the rest of us sat in the same places, with Iris in Iris's chair rather than Vi. Traudy was wearing the same white cardigan draped over her shoulders.

Our mother was the first to sit down. As soon as she was settled, she said, "It was so nice of Vi to make us dinner last night."

"I know," said Iris. "She must be very lonely if she spends so much time with us old fogies. Doesn't she ever get to see that nice young husband of hers?"

"I don't see how she can," said our mother.

"He's very attractive, don't you think?"

"Oh, yes," said our mother.

"Don't you think so, Charles?" Iris persisted. She was passing Budge the shrimp salad.

"That's your department, not mine," he said.

"I understand he's very successful," said Iris. She blotted her upper lip with several soft pats of her napkin. One thing I will say for our poor squirrel-infested house in the Berkshires—it never got this hot.

"What exactly does he do?" I asked, able to talk more easily to her now that I was serving myself shrimp.

"He's a shopping consultant," said Charles.

"I believe the usual term is 'investment counselor,' " said Iris.

"He tells people whether or not to go ahead and buy that ski house in Vail," said Charles. "Well, I suppose someone's got to lead those people's lives for them."

It annoyed me that when Charles was in the room, the tendency was still to look at him rather than Iris. Of course he did have that huge white jutting forehead and those shadowy eyes, but it wasn't so much his appearance that attracted attention. It was more that he was perfectly at ease when people looked at him. Iris, even after a year of her new career, resisted attention as much as she courted it. She still sat in the straight, strict way that implied an audience of thousands, but her eyes were always trained on Charles, and I found mine slipping that way, too.

"Is Vi going up to Cold Spring this weekend?" asked Iris.

Budge said that she was.

"How nice," said Iris.

I noticed that Charles was already on his seconds.

"Joan might stay here," said our mother, although I'd told her earlier that I most decidedly would.

"You're not coming?" said Budge. "There are baby bunnies down the road. Just two weeks old."

"Joan doesn't get to see much of her mother," said Iris.

"Neither do I," said Budge.

"I wonder how Vi can get away so often," said our mother, and Iris said, "Curious, isn't it?"

I don't know what I'd expected from Iris's new incarnation. I blurted out: "You don't seem any different, really."

Iris considered this, which I found flattering. Sometimes I got the idea that kids were the only ones with anything left to think about. "I was not as disappointed with my first year as some of the other freshmen," she said. "But I don't think I have the unrealistic expectations some people do. I've never been particularly happy."

"Oh, Mummy," said Budge, "you're happy," and Charles said, "The Spinneys have wills of iron. They always get what they want."

This was a new slant on our mother, and one that struck me offhand as true, although I may have liked it because it meant I didn't have to worry about her. Our mother, on the other hand, didn't seem to realize that Charles had been referring to her, too. She said to Iris, "Oh, yes! You've done so much! Tell Joan how they adopted your language for the patients' rights bill!"

"I just wanted mental patients to know what they were giving up—and what they weren't—when they were committed. It's appalling what goes on in some of those places."

"They need better men at the public institutions," said Charles. "Putting some words on a piece of paper isn't going to change that any."

"I'm talking about some of the most expensive asylums, as well," said Iris. "I paid a visit to the most beautiful old Victorian mansion near Poughkeepsie. I would never have noticed the bars on the windows if I hadn't been looking for them. The grounds were impeccably kept. There must have been a dozen different kinds of roses, and the shrubs were trimmed as evenly as crystal balls, and paths wound around everywhere. I felt such a sense of peace I would have gladly spent a weekend there. Yet even this lovely place was polluted. A doctor who had an affair with a patient actually sued for custody of the child."

"Children should have custody of themselves," I said.

"Well, this child is only one year old," said Iris. "But he's living with his father now. The mother had to agree not to contest the suit, or they'd have locked her up again."

"Did she have a hysterectomy?" said Charles in a serious voice, as if he were really afraid she had.

"Not that I know of," said Iris, puzzled.

"So why doesn't she have another kid? Certainly the sexual relationship that that would entail cannot be morally repugnant to her."

Iris folded her hands, one over the other. "I know you think you're being funny," she said. "But do you really think people are interchangeable?"

There was an awkward pause.

"I ask, because you sometimes behave as if they were," she continued.

"How come you always act like everything is so awful?" said Budge suddenly.

"Me?" said Iris.

"Well I don't mean the milkman," cried Budge. Her face was flushed.

"But what is so awful?" said Iris.

"All those awful people you talk about," said Budge. "I don't know why you had to become an assemblyman, anyway."

"And you were always the *good* one," said Traudy with some satisfaction, speaking for the first time during the meal.

Fortunately the phone rang then. If kids knew how they really behaved with their parents they wouldn't let the witnesses live. But I don't think they notice. The petulance, neediness, and horrifying honesty come all too naturally. (Hugh and I were different. Since our parents weren't parents, we were awful to them mainly by not talking at all.)

"I don't think I like your tone of voice," said Charles, but by that time everyone was distracted. Traudy announced that the call was for me, and I was afraid it was going to be our father.

It turned out to be Aaron. "Remember me?" he said.

"How are you?" I said, wondering how much of my part of the conversation could be heard in the dining room.

"Impatient," he said. "Do you think you could sneak out of there?"

"I doubt it," I said. The phone was just inside the kitchen on a little built-in desk topped with five pigeonholes. I was standing with my profile to the dining room so I could see Iris—and Traudy's back—out of the corner of my eye.

"I keep thinking about you," he said.

This sounded a little more promising. "Oh, really?"

"I've never made it with a mother and a daughter," he said.

I made a humming sound in the back of my throat.

"You don't have to get stuffy," he said. "I don't mean at the same time."

This I didn't respond to at all. I was insulted he hadn't bothered to compliment me personally.

"We never got to smoke that grass this afternoon," he said. "How about I show you the sights tomorrow?"

"I have stuff to do," I said.

His voice got a little harder. "How would you like it if I told your mother what you did today?"

"Go ahead," I said. For the first time in the conversation, I was surprised. Did he really think such a threat would work? He couldn't have been that stupid.

He pressed on. "What would she think of you then?"

"I don't know," I said. "Would you like me to get her?"

"Come on, Joan," he said. "Don't be like that."

"Hang on a second." I dropped the receiver on a small pad of paper with the word SOAP printed on it in pencil and went into the dining room to get our mother. "It's Aaron Lemon," I said. "He wants to talk to you."

"Did you tell him we were eating?" said Charles.

"I'll tell him I'll call back," said our mother. "I can't imagine what he's calling *here* for."

I started in on my shrimp again; everyone else was finished.

"We're having strawberry shortcake for dessert," said Iris brightly.

"Mmm," I said, looking at Budge, who evidently was no longer speaking.

Our mother came in and said, "Iris's strawberry shortcake may be my favorite dessert in the whole world."

"What did that Lemon character want?" said Charles.

"Oh," said our mother, as if she didn't want to be bothered with the subject. "He wanted permission to take Joan to the Statue of Liberty tomorrow." Then she said to me, "You know you don't have to get my permission for anything. I'm not going to say no."

I kept eating.

Traudy said to me, "I hope he behaved himself today."

"Aaron?" said our mother. "He may not be the sort of person you're used to, but he's all right."

"I'm sure he is," said Traudy. "But I got a funny feeling about him, and it's better to be safe than sorry."

"Who's Aaron?" asked Iris.

"You remember," said our mother. "Budge called him the 'Big Dandelion.' "

"I did?" said Budge.

"This guy is just a kid," said Traudy.

"Your dates are always so young," said Iris to our mother.

Traudy folded her lips in a thin line. "He looks like he lives off his parents."

"I don't think he does," said our mother. "He's a musician."

"Has Joan made a conquest?" asked Iris.

"The Statue of Liberty—yuck," said Budge.

"Actually, Cold Spring sounds like a lot more fun," I said, and immediately felt great relief.

"We'll have a wonderful time," said Budge.

"You can help keep Vi out of trouble," said Iris.

"If only I could go, then everything would be perfect," said our mother.

I had once, when I was six or seven, spent a week at the house in Cold Spring with Iris and Polly and Budge. And Traudy, of course. And our grandmother, who didn't stay in the main house with the rest of us, but in a guest house across the street, near the tennis courts. I had few memories of the visit, but I did remember the tunnel-like route up the hill to the house. The dirt road was narrow and rocky, and the crowns of the trees melded overhead. Without any sky, the road was like a hall; the spaces between the trees for the occasional driveway were as narrow as doors; and the clearings opening up behind them, for the houses, were as small and discrete as rooms.

As the car climbed the hill this time, crunching and popping noises came from under the tires, and I felt a bit of the same lift I had as a child.

"I miss your mother already," said Vi, turning around in the seat to speak to Budge. It was one of those new seats that silhouetted a person's head and body, so Vi had to lean over toward Charles and poke her incongruously sharp nose around the fresh blue-gray vinyl. The posture seemed to me a very intimate one.

At first, when we'd picked her up on Park Avenue, outside the huge canvas-colored building where she and J.J. lived, Budge had been up in the front seat, and Vi had started to climb into the backseat with me. Charles, showing unusual restraint, ventured no opinion, but fortunately Budge sprang out of the front seat and slipped into the back, all the while murmuring, "Oh, Vi, how nice to see you," and the like.

Vi was carrying a small black leather suitcase something like a doctor's bag and a much larger, paper bag–covered bundle wound with string, which she set upright on the floor in front of her. "Don't you want to know what this is?" she said to Charles.

"Okay, what is it?" he said.

"It's a surprise," she said, and Charles didn't seem to mind at all. He laughed a little. Vi made several references to the present on the rest of the trip. It was going to need some "TLC"; it would never be as beautiful as the house was already; it was really for Iris. On that last road on the hill, as we jounced back and forth, I noticed that she was steadying the package between her knees.

The Eberlanders' house was at the highest point in the road, before it started to curve down again. The house itself was in two parts. There was a large, rough-hewn hunting lodge–like first floor and then a smaller, wackier, ski lodge–like second floor, which had odd windows (an L-shaped one hugged a corner) and a modern-day widow's walk on the side facing the river.

Charles disappeared inside with his overnight bag before the rest of us even got out of the car. Vi and Budge seemed to be in no hurry. They left their suitcases (and the package) and wandered out to the wide cedar deck in back, where they sat down on chairs made of dozens of white rubber ropes and looked absently into the kidney-shaped pool. For some reason I followed them with my suitcase, which was too big and had scratches all over it, like an old floor.

"You don't have to guard your stuff here," said Budge, and I wondered why on earth I'd come.

She and Vi seemed to be waiting for something, and sure enough, within minutes, Charles appeared at the sliding door in a baggy green plaid bathing suit gathered by a white drawstring. Without pausing, he dove in one side, swam underwater the length of the pool, and popped up on the other side, with a great doglike shaking of the short hairs on his head. "Let the festivities begin!" he shouted.

"He always does that," said Budge.

"He always says that, too," added Vi.

"Who's joining me?" he said, floating away from the wall on his side. "Budge?"

"Too cold," she said.

"Nonsense," he said. "Vi?"

"I have to get hot first."

"Joan?" But this was said in a way that did not seem to require a response.

Vi said to Budge, "I suppose you want to sleep with your cousin tonight." To me she said, "I slept in Budge's room last time, and we talked until three o'clock. It was so much fun, just like a slumber party."

"I told her lots of ghost stories," said Budge.

Vi gave an exaggerated shiver. She was acting more childishly than Budge.

We were maybe three quarters of a mile up the side of a very large hill, and below us were two bends of the wide, flat, shiny Hudson River. The deck jutted straight out in the back of the house, so that although trees loomed on either side of us, we were in effect suspended over the greenery between us and the river. Through the cracks in the cedar floor I could see a sort of lawn, some scraggly ivy, and a mass of evergreens sloping away into invisibility. The deck was immaculate in comparison: Every few feet there were pink begonias in brass-handled cedar tubs, and the smell of chlorine was as sharp as that of fresh mimeos.

"You're a bunch of old fuddy-duddies," called Charles as we moved off into the house, Budge and Vi going around the front to pick up their bags and me pushing my embarrassing suitcase over the tracks of the sliding door. This was the dining room, where there were three Hudson River paintings, all of which seemed to be of the same mountain, the same bend in the river (not one of those you could see from the house), and the same tall, bulging oak trees. Three walls in the room were wood; the fourth was actually the stone back of the fireplace in the living room, with open spaces on each side. In the living room, which was two stories high, there were more Hudson River paintings, one showing white boats in the water threatened by a storm. This was the one painted by a famous artist.

I heard Budge say to Vi at the mudroom door, "You always cheer him up."

In the upper, ski lodge–like part of the house was the top of the living room and also the master bedroom, which was directly above the dining room, kitchen, mudroom, and hall—it was huge. In fact, it was at least five times bigger than any of the other bedrooms, which were lined up crookedly off the kitchen. Vi said, "I'll take the sink room," referring to the antique sink set in the top of a dresser that had always been in the farthest room. I remembered pink shells painted on the rim.

Budge threw her bag on one of the twin beds in her room. "Let's go for a hike," she said, which cheered me instantly—I figured we could get away and smoke my joints—but then she went into the sink room and asked the same thing of Vi. So all three of us were going. Obviously it was going to be a real hike.

Charles was out of the pool by then, lying on the chaise longue, wearing a pale yellow shirt, and reading a psychoanalytic journal. He said, "Watch out for the wolves."

This odd remark soon made me think that even he would have fit in better on this hike than I did. Stuff I couldn't understand would set Vi and Budge off into fits of giggles. Sometimes one of them would have to stop to lean against a tree. And this was a woman of—well, I didn't know how old Vi was, but she was probably about thirty-five. They would both slip into this curious way of talking, half Hungarian accent and half baby talk, which for some reason involved referring to themselves in the third person. I thought maybe it was just something rich girls did, but it made me uncomfortable. I couldn't in a million years try it myself; at the same time I felt that I ought to—that I was being a drip. So I smiled with exaggerated good humor every time either of them addressed me, and we walked on and on.

When we got back, Vi unwrapped her surprise, which was a small, blossomless lilac bush; it looked like a handful of pussy willows, actually. Charles said, "Oh, nice," and Vi briskly demanded shovel, hose, and potting soil.

I suppose this meant that Budge was left with me, but she took a bath, I read a mystery, and we barely spoke. Before dinner, when Budge was explaining the code Iris used on the food in the freezer, I heard the two of them slip into their baby talk in lieu of quarreling over whether a figure was a "2" or a "7." Either way, we wound up eating lasagna that Iris had made.

After dinner we went to the fireworks. As we drove past a number of quaint little stores and restaurants to get to a good viewing spot, it occurred to me that the Eberlanders had a "country" house in a town that was bigger than the one I lived in all the time. I was scowling out the back window when Charles mentioned that the fireworks were being set off across the river at West Point.

"West *Point*?" I said.

"I know exactly what you mean," said Vi, cocking her head to look back at me.

Vi always knew exactly what everyone meant, I noticed.

"What's wrong?" said Charles. "Don't you think we should have an army?"

"No," I said. "I don't." I was still looking out the window, letting my eye catch on individual trees as they flashed past.

"It certainly would be wonderful if it weren't necessary," said Vi.

"That is the most incredible swill I have ever heard!" Charles was as impassioned as if he had been personally offended. The tone startled me (what was he doing, yelling at a fifteen-year-old girl about this?), and even frightened me a little.

"Now, Charles," said Vi with a gentle reprimand. "We just don't want to feel we're condoning war crimes."

I expected a further explosion, but Vi obviously had had a lot of practice dealing with him. He said, "Next time we'll go to the pacifists' fireworks," and she giggled.

Actually, West Point turned out to be everything I could have hoped. It rose darkly from the trees on the other side of the Hudson like some medieval prison. Mostly it was all blank stone walls outfitted with a fringe of crenallations and towers and a few small, protected arches. And in each wall, high above the rugged shoreline below, was a single slit of a window. I mean, it was truly gothic.

We parked next to a van painted with white clouds, black peace signs, orange daisies, purple balloon letters (LOVE and EAT MEN, obviously changed from EAT ME), zodiac signs in various colors, and a huge red, white, and blue rainbow. The van was the kind with windows in the back, and inside you could see some sleeping bags and clothes and unidentifiable pieces of fabric all in a big tangle. An incredible lust rose in me. Oh, to have such a van, with some like-minded friends, out on the road—it seemed to me freedom as I'd never known it. The trouble was, the van would probably turn out to be owned by someone like Aaron Lemon.

Still, I hoped that Charles would be somewhat abashed by the sight. Instead, he said, "I see *they* aren't afraid of a little red, white, and blue."

He chose a spot in a thin little park on the other side of the train station, near a gazebo and under a weeping willow. All around us people sat on blankets, listened to transistor radios, and rummaged in coolers. The van was obviously not an anomaly: Most of the crowd was young and wore torn jeans and sandals and headbands. As night fell, I saw the quick thickenings of light that signaled joints being passed. No one else seemed to care that we were facing this living emblem of the military-industrial complex.

The four of us were sitting in a row: Charles and Vi on an old railroad tie and then Budge and me in the grass. I couldn't hear what Charles was saying, but I kept hearing Vi giggle. Sometimes I heard both her and Budge giggle. I tried to disassociate myself from them by leaning farther and farther away, widening the gap between us. The one thing Budge said to me—"Can you see?"—I answered with a discouraging monosyllable. I was sure that Polly would never be this embarrassing with Vi.

I got to thinking about Charles and Vi as the first fireworks blossomed in the sky. Fireworks were like smoking dope—supposedly something exciting in and of itself was happening, but actually what it did was loosen and then focus your mind in a truly wonderful way.

Kids I'd always figured you could gauge by certain key qualities: Boys mastered a situation by being "funny," girls did it by being perky. I could outline in my school a sort of solar system for each sex. In one center was a funny boy who was also widely admired, who was sexually experienced, who at at least looked like he could run or play ball or fight. Then there was the funny boy who was maybe a quieter, skinnier version of the center, the funny boy who was maybe a little sloppier, the funny boy who was good at something weird like golf, and the funny boy who was not taken seriously as a date or even a friend (and who was probably the only truly funny one).

The center of the girl's solar system was beautiful as well as perky, but beauty alone was not enough, maybe because perkiness was a measure of receptivity to boys. The most beautiful girl in my class was so painfully sweet and quiet and shy, I had heard her speak only a handful of times. Ronnie was very, very perky: close to the center. I was in sort of a medium level of perkiness. Leila wasn't perky at all, but she was far too cool for it to matter. Yet these structures seemed universal. Certainly there was an equivalent solar system of the hoodier boys; I noticed because I was keenly aware of its sun, a wrong-side-of-the-tracks type who could send my heart backflipping down the hall.

Charles I could see as a center of sorts, assuming his brand of barbed remark was a grown-up version of funniness. And Vi was certainly much perkier than Iris; in that sense Charles belonged with Vi. But I figured Iris was something like my best friend, although maybe even farther off the map, considering all her brushes with death and the like. Besides, here at the Eberlanders', the system seemed to break down. Polly and Budge were exremely perky, but only for grown-ups—Polly's perkiness, at least, being a complete counterfeit. Where did they fit?

We all went to our rooms that night at about the same time, and Budge fell asleep almost immediately. I lay awake and listened for footsteps either into or out of Vi's bedroom. Every once in a while I could hear a creak in a board, but nothing measured itself out into steps, and eventually I, too, dropped off to sleep.

Budge was gone when I woke up. I lay in bed, again listening for sounds, but soon gave up and wandered out to the deck, where I found Vi just starting to put on her suntan lotion. "Charles and Budge have gone into town to pick up some food," she said.

First she squirted a long line of lotion down each arm and started to rub it in, causing a slight wrinkling and quivering in the flesh. Then she squirted some lotion on the palm of her hand and massaged it into her neck and chest, leaning forward so that the breasts cupped by the top of her bathing suit elongated a little. There were freckles sprinkled over her breastbone. She raised one knee as she put lotion on her stomach; her belly button winked as the slab of skin it was embedded in was stretched up and down. Then she started under her raised thigh, which looked huge to me, although she was a normal-size woman. Her legs were dotted where grown-up hairs had been shaved away; her kneecaps stood out as white as scar tissue; and her feet were very long and bony, with thick, heavy ridges in the nails.

It hit me that this was a body in a way that a teenage body was not. On Budge, clothes, skin, and bone were all one smooth, firm unit, as if she were a picture of a person in a magazine. On Vi, there was real flesh that was somehow alarmingly separate and alive, with its quivering and winking and stretching. It had been used for things, I thought—lots of things. It scared me. "Do my back?" she said in that pleasant, smiling way of hers, and she turned in the chaise longue, so that she was half twisted in front of me. I stood over her to squirt some lotion between her shoulder blades; it smelled like the beach. She was wearing some kind of musky perfume, too, and underneath I thought I could distinguish the damp fresh scent of her sweat. Muscles started rippling under her skin as I rubbed the lotion in: She was shrugging the bathing-suit straps off her shoulders.

"You like Iris very much, don't you?" she said. My hand was at the meeting of her neck and shoulder when she spoke. Charles had put his hand there. In fact, for a brief, brain-fibrillating moment, my hand felt like his hand. It was the first time I'd had any sense of what an affair between Charles and Vi might mean, and I was shaken when I said, "Yes, I like Iris."

It's not that I wasn't used to a theoretical, anything-is-possible sort of sexual realm. This was the realm in which the Eberlander dinner conversation took place, after all. Hadn't I heard Charles make penis envy and anal fixations and even vaginal orgasms sound like phrases from a textbook for as far back as I could remember? This was also the realm in which Leila and I would go through every male of our acquaintance, deciding whether we would go "all the way" with him. (A surprising number passed, considering we were virgins. We both swore, however, that we were just waiting for someone who knew what he was doing.) Real sex, having been confined to deep squeezings and rubbings in between kisses, reminded me a little of musical chairs; twice I'd done it in a larger tangle of both boys and girls. Our "orgies" we called them. Even Ronnie sleeping with her English teacher seemed faintly theoretical, perhaps because it involved school.

In this sense I could understand Charles and Vi: He was a male, she was a female, they were both consenting adults, and I didn't believe in marriage, anyway. I was unprejudiced and sensible. But to think of his hand on her shoulder, her hand on his chest, his clothes *off,* well . . . ; her flesh exposed, his mouth open, her legs raised, his *dick,* well . . .

"Teenagers nowadays have a much healthier attitude toward sex than we ever did," said Vi.

I didn't trust myself to speak. I went back to the kitchen for some toast. Later I changed into my bathing suit, managing to stay in the bedroom until I heard the sound of the car in the driveway.

"Come on," said Charles impatiently, as I emerged from the hall. Budge was opening the refrigerator door to put a carton of milk inside.

"Hold your horses, Tonto," she said.

I followed her down the hall, but she shut the door on me, so I went back and looked vaguely into the bag of groceries.

What I could see were two different kinds of pastries in boxes and a package of real butter. Then I went out and sat down one seat over from Vi, and there they were, both Eberlanders, in their suits. They stood for a moment at the deep end of the pool. Budge rattled her arms and pulled her suit down in back with one flick of an index finger. Charles inflated his chest. They both dove in, swam the pool underwater, and came up shaking and sputtering, each accusing the other of being too fast off the mark. Then Charles clambered out. Budge, who stayed in the pool, called, "Oh, Jo-oan, Jo-oan."

"In a minute," I said.

Charles dragged one of the lawn chairs closer to Vi, who was lying on her back now, her eyes closed. "What do you think?" she asked.

He said nothing.

"Of the article," she said. She giggled.

He said, "I think he'd like to get rid of drives altogether," and I closed my eyes.

"That's so true," she said.

Charles's words floated out over me, disembodied. "The whole crew is like that," he said. "They don't like mess. They are strictly professional men. They want the house in the country, the private schools, the nice vacations, the clean-cut kids. They should have become corporate lawyers. Or doctors in a nice safe specialty like radiology. No bothersome calls from patients."

"I know exactly what you mean," said Vi.

"Nesselroth has no passion," said Charles.

I had never pictured our uncle in quite this swashbuckling way before. I opened my eyes a slit. He was now bent a little over Vi, who still hadn't moved. When you thought about it, there was something incredibly suggestive about such a tall, bald forehead as his.

"He has no thirst for knowledge," said Charles.

Plus his knuckles were too thick and round for his fingers. In a flash I thought about what it would be like to be crushed under the weight of a grown man. I turned over on my stomach and picked up my mystery.

"I don't think he was really analyzable. I made a big mistake, letting Booker take him on."

I wondered why I had never realized how sexual a mad scientist really was. I remembered Jane Fonda strapped into that rippling machine in *Barbarella.* In my mystery I read, "She spun 'round and 'round, as if turned by giant hands."

Vi stirred and murmured, "It's a classic Oedipal conflict."

Charles said, "I know he expects to become a training analyst. He thinks of it only in terms of the status it will confer. He thinks it's his due. But the idea of his training others is absurd. He has no vision."

In the pause I read, "The water inched up her body. Her flesh anticipated every rise. Her skin seemed to ache with the fear of it."

Vi said, "He blames you for everything because he thinks you're all-powerful. In fact, he really thinks you're perfect."

I was thinking of being hosed off: here, there, oh, how delicious. I jumped up, banged my book shut, and practically fell into the pool.

Budge eyed me, glistening, as I came to the surface. "Whoa, Nelly," she said, holding on to the edge of the pool as if she would be swept away. "What jumping beans got into you?"

Vi made lunch by putting things together that would have been perfectly all right left apart: She speared scoops of tunafish salad with celery, she put orange wedges on lettuce, she mixed ginger ale and Hawaiian punch for us to drink. Afterward, she and Charles went for a hike, which I was relieved to see I wasn't expected to join. As soon as they'd left, Budge said that Charles could make anything—even a walk in the woods—seem like something you were being forced to do against your will.

I finally brought out my joints, but Budge was afraid to smoke them in the house because of the smell, and afraid to smoke them outside because she wasn't sure where her father would be walking. Her worries made me feel bolder; I made her admire my craftsmanship. Maybe I was a little smug. She said, "I suppose we could go down to the guest house," adding later, "You don't know what it's like because your mother is so hip."

"Oh, I don't know," I said. At this point we were picking our way down the steep dirt driveway at a companionable sort of pace.

"All you have to do is look at her," said Budge. "I couldn't believe it when she said at dinner that you could do anything you wanted. She's a real person, almost like Vi."

"Mmm," I said.

"You can talk to her about anything," said Budge.

"Actually, it's our father who smokes dope," I said.

"You're kidding."

"No." It was funny, how much more comfortable I was talking about such things in the woods than I was on the city streets. But then I was used to wandering around the woods.

"That's so wild. My father would die first."

"You really think he's never tried it?"

"I'm sure of it."

"It's always kind of hard to picture your parents, you know, having sex or whatever."

"Yuck," said Budge.

"I know what you mean," I said.

"As far as I'm concerned, they did it twice."

"Twice," I said, shaking my head in disbelief. "Hugh and I are probably virgin births."

By then we were at the gate on the road to the guest house. A chain had been strung around it twice and fixed with a padlock. "It's locked," I said.

"That's just for people driving by, not us," said Budge, without breaking her stride. I followed her down what soon became a path next to the chain-link fence. Eventually the fence stopped amid a thicket of trees, and the path doubled back on the other side. We were making a great deal of noise, crashing through dry leaves, popping sticks, and sweeping past overgrown bushes. I could barely hear Budge when she said, "Did you really *see* your father smoke dope?"

"It was at the dinner table."

Budge covered her mouth and squealed.

"It was sort of embarrassing, really."

Budge turned around to face me. "Sometimes my father will say something very Freudian to someone I know, who'll say, 'Wow, your father's cool,' totally not getting it."

"Yeah."

"I mean, he is the most straightlaced person in the world."

The guest house came into sight then: a small gray clapboard cabin with a screened-in porch. It was the oldest house on the hill, and when the Eberlanders bought it to prevent the land from being developed, they planned to raze it to avoid paying the property taxes. Instead, they ended up putting in new plumbing and a new roof. The screens had been new the last summer I was there. The place hadn't changed much since, except that foliage had grown up and around the porch, so it looked more hidden than I remembered it. An oak bough scratched a screen a little in the breeze. The tennis courts, too, were hidden. I think that as soon as I saw that new foliage, and the quiet, empty gray porch, and the slightly warped screen door that supposedly hadn't been opened in weeks, I knew what we would find.

But I kept walking. I said nothing. Oftentimes, there was nothing to be said. Sometimes I could rely on the political thinkers I admired. Other times my head would get so jammed, there was no unblocking it. There was no way to relate C. Wright Mills to that walk toward the porch.

Budge had said that her father was straightlaced, which was obviously not true, but, despite my assumptions about him and Vi, I knew that it wasn't completely wrong, either. The words just didn't fit; they fell through the net. The sixties had finally given Hugh and me a language to explain what had happened to our parents: Our mother had gone off to "find herself" before it became fashionable; our father had "dropped out" years ago. It was comforting to imply that the rest of the world had finally caught up with them. But I knew that the truth was sadder, odder, scarier. It was like a species of animal that had always lived deep in a labyrinth of caves. Or a species of fish that had always lived on the bottom of the ocean far from the reach of sunlight. It didn't look like anything else.

Weeds had grown up almost level with the gray wood steps. On the porch were two basket chairs painted dark green. The print on the seat cushions had faded into obscurity. (Flowers, maybe? Pinecones?) A small spiderweb linked a jutting thermometer to the window. Everything had that faint, damp, cast-off smell. The door inside stuck a little, and Budge gave it a smart rap with her knee.

"Polly and I were never allowed to stay here by ourselves," said Budge as the door creaked open and a shade rattled against it. "And now it's hardly ever used. I don't know what happened to all my parents' friends."

The walls were surprisingly bright with knotty pine. Off to the left was an open kitchen, consisting of a sink, a stove, and a half-refrigerator. One cupboard door was partway open, and there was a glass half full of water on the table built for two. Off to the right was a woodstove with a couple of fawns—noses touching—molded into the doors. There was also an old hooked rug, a rocking chair, an end table made of a barrel, and a corduroy-covered divan. Tucked under the divan and hiking up the corduroy was a pair of men's shoes. Directly in front of me was the door to the bedroom, which was closed. I crossed the room to open it.

. . .

Budge is forty now and doesn't live too far from our father. It makes sense to stop by on my way up there, and every once in a while I do. She is such a thoroughly pleasant person. She and her husband and daughter live in a little white house anchored on one side by a massive red chimney. The town has some of the same scratchiness as the one I grew up in, but the inside of the house sets them apart: Everything is old and spindly and beautiful. Some of it came from the house in Brooklyn Heights when that broke up. She has the cabinet with the famous hand-painted doors. She has the mirror entwined with serpents. She has the big blue bowl. It seems a nice place to stop for a quick drink.

So I call up Budge, and her voice is always the same: So warm and pleased, it makes me wonder why I've put off seeing her for so long. Her husband gets out some crackers and cheese—he's the one who does the cooking—and we sit in the living room "to really *talk,*" says Budge. I like a place where the wood floor gleams. So I ask her how she's been and she says fine and she asks how I've been and I say fine except I'm furious at someone, always—a pollster misrepresenting the senator I work for, a columnist who misquoted her, a colleague who double-crossed her—which makes Budge retreat a little. She says, "Your job always sounds so exciting." I tell her how polls can be slanted—or quotes doctored or whatever—and she says, "It's always so nice to see you again," and I say, "Yes, yes, wonderful," and try to tell her about the terrible traffic or the ridiculous detour on my trip up, but when I pause she says, "You must be so proud of your brother" (for whatever mathematics prize he has just received), so I say, "Of course, of course," and her husband says something like how their daughter uses "on" and "off" interchangeably, which I could actually add to, because I also have kids who do cute stuff, but then Budge says, "Isn't it wonderful, how many good things can still happen? Isn't life amazing?" So I tell her for the one thousandth time how much Iris's example meant to me, and Budge smiles her big smile and says, "I'm so glad." I always forget how defeating those words (*happy, glad*) can be.

It's as if only the false front is left. She grew into it, of course; it doesn't sound as wrong as it did on a fifteen-year-old kid, but all complications were knocked right out of her, as far as I could tell. After a while, though, I forget this, and I start to think, Look what I did to her that day; and, What's so bad about enthusiasm and good manners? I get to thinking that I'll stop by again when I have a chance, and the whole process starts over.

I sensed something of this as I opened the bedroom door that day. The future was there, as real as the click the tongue made as it withdrew. I could feel it: I felt it in my legs, in my arms, and especially in my fingers as they lay oh so lightly on the rough wooden knob. I knew I was dividing Budge's life in two the way mine had been divided in two when I learned that our mother was leaving. I had gone into the house and then looked back outside through the window at the empty road. Behind me was one life; ahead of me was another. And although of course no details rose before my eyes, I felt for a moment every emotion I was ever going to run into for the rest of my life, and each one was new and strange. Whenever I have a sensation of déjà vu now, I assume I am reliving one of the great wash of things I felt at that time.

When I opened the door, Charles and Vi were standing in the middle of the room. They were dressed—we had, after all, made plenty of noise—but their faces were white and scared, and Charles had instinctively thrown his arm in front of Vi, as if they were in a car about to crash.

Then the front door slammed behind me, and Charles's face filled with the sort of darker emotions I was used to—anger, mainly. I began to think I'd imagined the fear. Certainly I myself was afraid, though not as much as you'd expect, since I still had this feeling of being seized by the future. "What do you think you're doing?" roared Charles, but Vi was already calling, "Budge! Budge!"

"Where did she go?" asked Charles.

I said I didn't know.

"She may have gotten the wrong impression . . ."

"You mean you're afraid she got the *right* impression," said Vi gently, but when Charles's face got blacker, she added, "Oh, why don't you go put on your shoes?"

There was no sign of Budge anywhere outside, and the woods had a hooded, unfriendly look. Vi kept calling her name. I sat on the steps with my hands in my pockets until Charles brushed past me, saying, "Why are you always just hanging around? Can't you think of anything to do?" To Vi he said, "I'm going up to the house and make sure her money is still there."

"He's very worried," she said to me, as if apologizing for his behavior. Perhaps because of this, we drifted together in his wake and followed him up the dusty dirt road. He had left the gate open, the chain dangling, and the padlock lying on the ground. As Vi was rethreading the chain, Charles reappeared, this time in the car. He rolled down the window and displayed my tangerine-colored, mirror-studded pocketbook, which, because of the way he held it, looked like a mere scrap of cloth.

"That's mine," I said, grabbing for it. At least I had the joints in my back pocket.

"I didn't *think* it was Budge's," he said with some contempt.

"Budge didn't bring a purse," I said.

"You look around and see what you can find," he said to Vi before driving off.

"Men always think they can solve things by getting into a car," said Vi, looking after him.

When we got to the house, she said she hated to go through Budge's things, but I noticed that this didn't even make her hesitate. All the clothes in Budge's suitcase were bright and crisp, even the underwear. In a side pocket were two silver barrettes and a key attached to a huge wooden "B." The bristles on her hairbrush were stuck into a rubber pad, so it looked sort of like a pet brush, except it was made out of tortoiseshell. A five-dollar bill was zipped into the overflap. On the dresser were her sunglasses and her thin, grandmotherly gold watch. At least the glasses were somewhat fashionable, with slightly tilted oval frames.

I said, "She could always hitchhike, if she wanted to get away."

Vi said, "Oh, God, don't tell Charles that. Let's hope she went up into the woods. You've got to go up the path we hiked yesterday. I don't know what would happen if I went. She might . . . she might hide. I'd afraid, you know, that she might be mad at me."

"Okay," I said numbly, although I was actually eager to get away.

Vi said, "Tell her she's my special friend."

That really was a dumb thing to say, I thought. On the other hand, you could see why Budge thought of her as a regular person. She was sitting there on Budge's star quilt, with her hands down between her knees, palms pressed out, and her nose looking even sharper than usual—the tip had turned white.

As I started up the path, I called, "Budge! Budge!" a couple of times, but I soon stopped. I walked maybe fifteen minutes, then sat on a stump and smoked a joint. It was upsetting to have felt that piratical pull toward a person I disliked as much as I did Charles. I wondered if Iris and Vi disliked him, too, but in a way that just added to the romantic image I'd had had a glimpse of earlier. It was a holdover from a past era, I was sure. There would be none of that when I was older and my life had finally opened up as it was supposed to. In the meantime, I felt as if I should have said something to Vi when she referred to the new attitude toward sex. It reminded me uncomfortably of the time our mother asked me, months before she left, how I would like it if we were on our own. I couldn't remember my reply, but clearly it hadn't been negative enough.

While I was thinking these things, I kept having to get up because I felt ants crawling on me. I never found any. Not having a watch, I couldn't tell how long I was there, but several times I thought I ought to go back and several times I thought better of it.

When I finally returned, Vi was still alone, sitting up sideways on the chaise longue on the deck and looking out into the woods. She called, "Anything?" and when I drew nearer, she said, "There's been nothing here." I was pretty hungry, but I figured it was easier just to nod and look grave and escape into the bedroom and read.

You'd think a house that had been around for as long as that one and that had had that much money poured into it could muffle the sense of disaster I recognized from my own house. It couldn't, though, perhaps because the Eberlanders had been camouflaging themselves with outsiders (me, among others), and now the outsiders were the only ones left. It seemed fitting that when Charles came back, it was Vi and me who had the heart-to-heart talk. Vi scratched on the bedroom door like a dog, then told me at great length how important it was that Budge be found, how worried Charles was, how she had told him I wasn't holding anything back, but how she just wanted to make sure, because finding Budge was so very, very important.

I said, "I know," in a kind of freezing way until she withdrew.

I had actually been left alone for a while when the phone rang. Charles answered it and almost immediately started barking out questions: "What do you mean, she's there? How did she get there? She doesn't have wings . . . Well, where did she get the money? They didn't let her ride for free . . . I don't care . . . *She's* upset! How do you think we feel?"

I crept out. If that was Iris on the other end, it didn't sound like she'd gotten any startling revelations about Charles's behavior.

"You can tell her from me, she's going to get the whaling of her life," said Charles. He was pacing up and down in front of the breakfront as Vi and I watched.

"Fine," he said. "That's fine with me. We'll be back in a few hours. It happens to be absolutely the worst time for traffic."

He hung up the phone with a clatter. "She's home," he said to Vi, who said, "How *did* she get there?"

"Train," he said. "Iris makes her carry a ten-dollar bill in her shoe. But what are you sitting there for? We've got to pack. You and Joan can take care of Budge's stuff. And if you forget something, it'll be just too damn bad for her."

Vi scuttled off. She did not seem surprised at being talked to that way, but I couldn't help thinking that maybe Charles had lost all his women in one blow: wife, mistress, daughters. Neither he nor Vi said much on the way back to Brooklyn. I kept watch, but I didn't see any hippie van or any other car that reminded me of freedom.

1970

My junior year I fell in with a new bunch of people who seemed to have come out of nowhere. One was a transfer student, one was a guy from the wrong side of town, two were a year younger. I suppose the others must have always been around. Anyway, we were all activists.

For the October moratorium we passed around word that a member of SDS would be speaking during the last period on the lawn in front of the school. Simply showing up was a protest, because it meant cutting a class. Far more students came than we expected—over fifty. One guy tried to lower the American flag, but he couldn't figure out how the pulley worked, and he was soon shouted down by some other kids nearby. I don't know how I would have reacted to actual vandalism. As it turned out, very few teachers reported us absent that period, and those students who were caught just got yelled at together down at the principal's office. I was one of them. Afterward he took me aside and said, "I'm glad nothing happened with the flag," and I shrugged my shoulders and said, "Well . . ." He wasn't a bad guy, I guess.

When we were planning for the November moratorium we decided we were too big for the high school. Five of us crammed into an old convertible and drove to Washington. I sat in the back the whole way. We all ate a bag of fried chicken I'd made, which was delicious. One guy kept singing, "And it's one, two, three, what are we driving for? Don't tell me, I don't give a damn, next stop is Framingham." I liked him—he insisted on watching the evening news upside down in his chair—but by the time we got to Pennsylvania, I was trying to make conversation to shut him up.

I had lost my virginity to the driver, Allen Earick, a couple of weeks earlier in a basement rec room, on a couch with an afghan throw. The afghan kept tickling my bare skin, but I didn't want to stop and move it, for fear I would look like I wasn't enjoying myself. Allen had said he wasn't in love with me because love was a bourgeois concept. I suspected there were other reasons, but that was all right with me; at least he knew what he was doing. The guy who'd said he was in love with me did not. It was all much less of a big deal than I'd figured. I analyzed it with my other political friends in a way I could never discuss what really happened to our mother.

Our father I could at least refer to in passing now. A senior who had his own rock band suddenly decided to take lessons from him, and once, when this breathtaking person was sitting around in our kitchen waiting, he said our father was "pretty hip." I was not as surprised as I would have been a year earlier. A newspaper boy had seen him smoking a joint in the backyard, and I figured word had gotten out. Also, Hugh and I never had curfews or anything, and after a while I noticed that this irregular sort of life gave us a status akin to the girls who already had college boyfriends. Or the boys who bought dope from real dealers instead of one another. Or the kids whose father owned a big mill in North Adams (though all they had to boast of were more and bigger versions of the same things everyone else had; they weren't like the Eberlanders).

Hugh went to a lot of tournaments, several at colleges. He won the one at Amherst. He was also Massachusetts Youth Champion. He took all of his books out of his bookcase and replaced them with trophies. He played in Albany, in Boston, in Hartford. When he played in New Haven in May, he wore a FREE BOBBY SEALE armband that I'd made for him.

A few days later, four students were gunned down at Kent State, and Albany, which had been pretty dead 'til then, went wild. I remember Allen pulling me out of study hall because he'd just heard on the car radio that hundreds of college students were lying down in front of a tollbooth on the highway. The next morning we were in Albany, too, marching with thousands of them down the center of one of the main streets. I was not a small person, but everyone seemed to be a little taller than we were, as well as a little older. Allen worked himself into what looked like a pretend rage and screamed, "Join us! Don't you care?" at a young guy standing on a curb. The guy was wearing an undershirt—kind of thin and grayish—instead of a real T-shirt, and I figured there'd be a fight unless I could successfully ignore the possibility. Sure enough, when I kept walking, Allen was soon trotting up beside me. Everyone surged up toward the Capitol and into the park in front.

The Capitol is a huge, chateaulike building set into a very steep hill. Leading up to it are hundreds of wide stone steps that seem to bulge out above you. They're cut too steep, and they undulate into steeper parts. Most people enter through the side rather than the front. In fact, I had never seen anyone on those stairs before that day, and the perspective is so off, it is hard to gaze up at them. The building sits above all this the way a person does on a rearing horse.

The park at the base of the steps is just a little sloped circle, ridiculously small next to them. Allen and I stood on a slanting sidewalk nearby, but I didn't feel as tilted as usual—it was if I were supported by the crowd—and even the overflow of people on the stairs seemed buttressed by all the bodies below.

Although I had never seen Iris's office, I knew it was on one of the upper floors. I toyed for the first time with the idea of stopping by, but it would have been difficult to get around to the side, and with Allen—well, it just seemed impossible. We were close enough to see the smoke when Nixon was burned in effigy on the statue of Sherman, and the idea of Iris's watching the fire made the top of my head warm. I felt self-conscious the way I had years earlier, when our grandfather had died, and I'd imagined him looking at everything I did. This was not a bad feeling, though. I thought what I was doing was terrifically interesting.

Our high school remained open through June, of course—unlike the colleges—but there were a lot of bomb scares on nice days. Then everyone would sit around on the front lawn, and you'd get to see all kinds of people who weren't in your classes. You could lie on your back in the grass. It was the most purely free time I ever knew. You couldn't do anything because you hadn't had the chance to plan for it. Sometimes I'd have a paperback with me. I can't look at my copy of *The Wretched of the Earth* now without smelling that spring air and feeling that old stir. I even know who called in one of the bomb threats. (It wasn't me.)

Sometime during that spring, our father got a phone call. We were having pancakes and sausages for dinner, and when the telephone rang, I was at the stove, turning over the second batch of pancakes. Hugh was at the kitchen table, eating the first batch with one hand and moving chess pieces with the other, a chess book propped open against a jar of applesauce in front of him. Our father had been watching the news, but he pounced on the phone before the second ring. He was like that; either he answered instantly or he ignored it altogether. "Iris," he said into the receiver, and then disappeared into the room with the piano, closing the door as much as he could around the corkscrewed telephone wire.

"Who was that?" asked Hugh.

"I think he said 'Iris.' "

"She's never called here in her life," said Hugh, returning to his book.

I had finished eating the second batch of pancakes by the time our father emerged. "She's a fine, fine woman," he said, pacing up and down after hanging up the receiver. "She and Charles are splitting up, and she is behaving like a thoroughbred. You can always measure people by the way they behave in a crisis, and she is the quality goods, one hundred percent. It's hard to believe that she and your mother were ever sisters."

I poured out the batter for a third batch of pancakes, and Hugh said, "They're getting *divorced*?" as if the very act were a shock and not something we lived with every day.

"Charles was having an affair. An affair! Can you believe it, when he had Iris Spinney!" Our father was still pacing back and forth, back and forth, right near the stove. If I'd turned suddenly, I could have caught him between the ribs with the spatula. "Even though I never liked him, I thought he had more sense than that."

"I don't believe it," said Hugh.

"She'll be better off in the long run," said our father. "I told her I was sorry. I think you have to. But I can tell that even she knows deep down how much better off she'll be."

"I thought they were really married," said Hugh.

"What does that mean?" said our father. "You think your mother and I weren't really married?"

Hugh scowled and looked down at his chessboard.

"I can't show you the marriage certificate," said our father, "because I tore it up. I was afraid of spontaneous combustion. But you think any marriage lasts these days? Don't kid yourself. Half-wits like your mother and Charles do anything they please."

I put the third batch of pancakes on the table, saying, "Maybe Iris left him. She certainly had reason."

But currying favor with our father rarely worked. "Nevah happen," he said, slurring his words for emphasis in a way that made my blood boil.

"Oh, yeah?" I said.

"Real women don't leave their marriages."

"What do you know about it?" Hugh shouted suddenly. "You don't know anything!"

"I know a hell of a lot more than you do," said our father in his steely voice. "You're too young to know what marriage means."

"I hate you! Every single one of you!" screamed Hugh.

Of course the divorce was more of a surprise for Hugh than it was for me. I'd never told him about the incident up at Cold Spring. In some odd way I felt as if I had the power to determine if it had happened at all. I'd expected a big blowup when we got back to Brooklyn, but once Charles dropped off Vi, she might as well never have existed. And Budge didn't seem to be around, either. That evening Charles and Iris came down to dinner as usual, and Charles told our mother he couldn't bear to look at those shaving commercials in which the razor is drawn against the direction the hair is growing. I still sometimes think about this when I shave my legs, because that is my method. I still don't know what's wrong with it.

Since I hadn't said anything about Cold Spring at first, I kept right on not saying anything. There was a point during the bus trip home when I might have broken my silence, but instead Hugh and I got to talking about why, if the Eberlanders were so rich, they lived on soup and sandwiches. I pretended to think they cut back whenever we were there and even argued this position with Hugh, although I knew it wasn't true. And after that—well, I certainly wasn't going to break our unspoken agreement in order to tell him something he wouldn't want to hear. It was our father who started to bring up the impending Fourth of July visit: "Tell Iris to get a good lawyer," he would say. Or, "Tell Iris I miss her."

. . .

As soon as Polly opened the door in Brooklyn Heights, I sensed the change: I could hear a faint wisp of Japanese flute melodies—the first music I'd ever heard played there. The walls had been painted a lighter color, and a lot of the heavier pieces of furniture had been replaced. There was no more dark green in the living room; the couch and chairs had all turned into various nubby tans and beiges. The round table with the thick cover was gone. I couldn't remember what the curtains had been like, but certainly they had not been made of this gauzy stuff.

Our mother was exclaiming, and Polly was saying, "How good to see you," and the like, all in that smooth way of hers, so I tried to get into the act, too.

"How wonderful to see you, Polly," I enthused. But as soon as the words were out, I knew they were a mistake. You can't have a conversation in which everyone talks like that. In a movie, say, you can understand what's going on if you see only one side of a conversation, but you can't be shown no sides at all.

"So how is everybody?" asked our mother, and Polly said, without changing her tone of voice, "Iris isn't feeling too good."

"What is it? What happened!" said our mother.

"Her rib cage is inflamed. She's resting now. Won't you sit down?"

We all sat.

"Can I get you something?" asked Polly.

"Oh, no, really, it's too much trouble," said our mother.

"It's no trouble," said Polly.

"No!" cried our mother. "Please!"

After a while Polly said, "Did you know that hives can be brought on by exposure to the sun?"

"That's right," said our mother. "She just got over that attack of hives."

We sat around like this until Traudy appeared in the doorway and said, "She wants you to come up."

So we all filed awkwardly into the master bedroom on the second floor—awkwardly because there is no way such a large group can be comfortable in a bedroom, especially if there is a pale, glittery-eyed woman smiling watchfully from the bed.

"Just don't make me laugh," she said. "I'm all right if I don't laugh."

"Oh, Iris," cried our mother. "I won't!"

"Don't, don't," she said, her arms wrapped around her chest as if to suffocate a chuckle. I had to look at the floor to keep from laughing with nervousness myself. Iris had gotten much slimmer. Because she had her eye makeup on even in bed, she looked like a sick person on a television show. She was wearing some kind of loose white textured silk robe, and the sheet and the eyelet cotton bedspread covering her were white as well. The bed ruffle was white. A fan slowly shook its head back and forth at us from a table by the window, making the café curtains billow out. They were white, too.

"I want you to know that this has not changed into a house of doom and gloom," said Iris. "We've been having tremendous fun, haven't we, Polly? We went to a Broadway play. We went to a dance concert where all the performers had pink brooms on their heads." Apparently even a thought like this was a danger: She kept her arms wrapped tight around her.

"We bought leather jackets," said Polly, sitting on the chaise longue. The rest of us were still standing.

"We ate ice cream cones," said Iris, as if to downplay the money angle. Then she changed tack. "Your cousin has grown into an incredibly handsome young man."

"Very handsome, indeed," said Polly, and I at least was grateful for her smooth manner, however fake. I was also aware of Hugh's physical presence in a way I never had been before. He had gotten taller and broader, and he looked less like our mother, because his face had lengthened. His blond hair stood up first and then dropped over his forehead like water spilling from a fountain—a careless, manly sort of look.

"What happened to your ribs?" he asked.

"The cartilage in between is swollen," said Iris. She suddenly bent over with a grimace, clutching her left breast with her hand. "No one knows what causes it."

"My God, Iris, how do you know it's not . . . serious?" said our mother.

"They did an EKG this morning," she said. "So they know it has nothing to do with my heart."

"Okay, I think you've had enough," said Traudy.

"No, no," said Iris, her face smooth again. "I'm all right. I just have to be absolutely still."

"Maybe it would be better . . ." said our mother.

"How was your trip?" asked Iris.

"There was a guy behind us talking about jail the whole time," said Hugh.

"How horrible," said our mother, hovering by the door.

"What did he say?" asked Polly.

Hugh shrugged. Actually, the guy had been bragging about how much money he'd made dealing there.

Iris turned her attention back to me. "The trouble is, you feel as if you can't breathe."

"Isn't there any medicine you can take?" I asked.

"They gave her a shot of cortisone," said Traudy.

"Right in the butt," said Polly, with a little social laugh.

"Polly was kicked out of school for having a boy in her room overnight," Iris said to Hugh.

Polly's face faltered for the first time.

Our mother jumped in. "She got into Sarah Lawrence anyway," she said.

"I think that kind of behavior is *encouraged* at college," said Iris.

But this suddenly was too much. She waved her hand at Traudy, who started to shoo us out. At the door, our mother said, "Is there anything I can do to help with dinner?"

"Traudy—" said Iris with her eyes closed.

"We'll worry about it downstairs," said Traudy.

That night our mother and I slept in Budge's room. (Polly's had only one bed.) I was lying on my side reading a book about Red China from one of the glassed bookcases in the dining room when our mother came in, sat on the other twin bed, and leaned forward in a way that warned me she was in a confiding mood. Soon she was saying, "It's amazing how much I can overlook because I want to believe the best about people. I hadn't a clue about Charles and Vi. But I think Iris must have known. It explains some things."

I dearly wanted to ask what things, but this was the sort of curiosity I never permitted myself with our parents. When she paused, I let my eyes drop back to my book. Then she continued, "Iris has been so great about it all. Charles says Joe Zigo is jealous; he and his ex-wife are sworn enemies."

I sat up. "You still see Charles?"

"Sometimes," she said. And then, as if to show there had been no betrayal, she added, "So does Iris."

"Iris sees Charles?" I echoed.

"They have dinner every few weeks. There's a lot to work out when you're getting a divorce."

Shortly after our mother left us, I dreamed that she came back. The relief that flooded through me was sharp, but temporary—even in a dream. I knew all about wish fulfillment, because of Charles, and the next morning I was ashamed of how pathetic the wish was. I knew perfectly well that our mother's return, if it were possible at all, would be no solution to anything. Four years later, as I lay on a twin bed ten feet away from her, I thought perhaps I should have dreamed instead that we suddenly got a lot of money. That did seem to make a difference. The disaster I'd expected up at Cold Spring still hadn't really happened.

I didn't see anyone when I came down for breakfast the next morning. I looked around a bit before I remembered that

Polly was taking French classes at NYU. (She needed the credits to graduate from boarding school.) I made myself two slices of toast and read a Pennysaver I found on the desk in the kitchen. The "Laughs" column was all about swinging singles. When I was halfway through it, Traudy stalked into the kitchen, put her hands on her hips, and said, "Your brother's up with Iris," and headed for the stairs. I took this as a sign I should follow her.

Hugh was sitting on Iris's bed with only a chess set between them. "If you move here, I move there, your queen has to drop back, and I move my bishop, pinning your rook against the king," he said, making the pieces fly.

Iris was as straight-backed as ever and so looked as if she were jammed up against the pillows instead of leaning on them. She had her old regal, slightly wry smile, she was on top of the white spread, and she was dressed. Her stockings were darker at the toes and heels. "Hugh is teaching me about chess," she said. "I don't know how he can keep all those pieces in his head."

Hugh was sitting with his chin in his hand, looking at the board. "Actually kids tend to be best at openings, when all the pieces are still there. That's what they study first. Then they play what is essentially a game of slaughter, leaving a king and a rook versus a king, or a king and a queen versus a king."

Hugh obviously did not consider himself in the "kid" category. But what category he did think he belonged to was not clear. He was certainly getting a kick out of sitting on Iris's bed. And they looked pretty together. Iris was so light and delicate now I almost wanted to pick her up or hug her or at least take her arm.

"Why aren't you at the McAlpin?" I asked with irritation.

Hugh looked at his watch. "They never start 'til late the first day."

"Aren't you at least supposed to register?" I asked.

"Since when do you care?" he said, but he was already pushing his pieces into the cardboard box and rolling up his plastic board.

"Oh, no! Tell me I haven't made you late!" said Iris.

I hadn't noticed the day before that this room had changed in a different way from the rest of the house. It was airy, like the downstairs, but there was something unfinished about it, too. Everything was arrested in mid-process. Sweaters were piled against the back of the chaise longue, next to which stood an unplugged floor lamp. A small, framed black-and-white photograph of some moss sat on the floor, leaning against the wall. One side of the bed was covered with papers: mimeos, tearsheets from magazines, and that sort of thing.

"How would you like to see the office?" said Iris when Hugh was gone. "You'd be doing me a big favor. I won't worry about collapsing if you're with me."

Of course I agreed, but when she swung herself up on my arm, I was surprised at the weight I was expected to bear: She must be really weak, I thought. I suggested she stay in bed, but she said the cortisone was working; and she did move more easily once she was on her feet.

I was proud to be seen walking with her on the street. Most of these people were her constituents, but they didn't seem to realize who was passing among them. This made me feel even more privileged, for some reason. I smiled at a couple of people we passed, which ordinarily I would never do. Iris walked very slowly, of course, but the effect was one of leisure and ease. We could have been walking arm-in-arm along a beach. A sweet cool breeze came in from the west.

As we turned the corner to the more commercial street her office was on, she said, "How is Polly, do you think?"

I was flattered, because this sounded like a real question, but of course there was nothing to say except "She's fine."

"I hope so," said Iris. "I know you haven't had an easy time, but I don't think divorce *has* to be too hard on the kids."

She unlocked the door with a key on a large, jingling ring. Her office had changed since the day of her primary victory. It looked more settled now. I could see only two phones. There were no big posters of her on the wall. Someone had left an old gray raincoat on a coat stand. I read everything I could while she went into the back room—a list of messages on one of the desks, an announcement of free outdoor concerts and an ad for a heating-oil reimbursement program, both on a bulletin board, a newsletter stacked on a nearly empty set of bookshelves. I stopped when I caught Iris watching me, though she seemed pleased. "My children don't care about this at all," she said.

"Oh, well," I said.

"You should come see me in Albany sometime."

"I was there right after Kent State," I said. "For the big march on the Capitol building."

"Oh," said Iris. She sat down suddenly, and the chair rolled a little on its coasters beneath her. "Let me think," she said. "I was giving a speech at a rally near Wall Street."

It had never surprised me that she held the political convictions she did, since I thought any clear-minded person would get to at least that stage. If she'd concentrated a little longer and harder, she'd have undoubtedly become more radical, but she was close enough; I thought it was great she'd been giving a speech. But I was sorry she hadn't been watching the demonstration I'd been in. I missed her, in retrospect, and I wanted to tell her, but I didn't know how. So instead, after a pause, I said, "I'm never going to get married."

"Oh?" said Iris. "Why do you say that?"

I looked down at the tops of my flip-flops. "Well, it doesn't seem to work out too well."

Iris laughed. "So what should we do about having kids?"

"On the kibbutzes in Israel, all the adults act as parents for all the children," I said promptly.

"So no kid gets stuck with a broken set?"

I hadn't thought of it quite like that, but I nodded.

"You can switch around at will?"

"I guess," I said. It was starting to sound a little silly.

Iris picked up a pen. "Your mother really misses you and Hugh," she said.

I looked at her.

"Not that that's something you have to worry about," she added.

I was ready to go, then. "I'm not worried about anything," I said.

That afternoon Polly and I were alone in the house, just having smoked a pipeful of hash out in the garden, when the phone rang. It was our mother, who asked if I wanted to go to the movie *Swaps.*

I made some kind of sound.

"Good," she said. "I'm going with Aaron. I'll get him to bring a friend."

"Aaron?" I said.

I was watching Polly slowly, slowly take a box of mint chocolate-chip ice cream out of the freezer. "What is it?" she said, and our mother said, "Was that Polly?"

"Yes," I said. Polly waved a second bowl at me in what must have been slow motion, and I nodded just as languidly: no-o-o-od, no-o-o-od. Then I lifted the receiver from my mouth and said, "We're going to go see *Swaps.*"

"Far out," said Polly. "Wasn't that the one the cardinal condemned?"

"Call you back later," said our mother, and hung up.

"I'll come, too," said Polly.

With our ice cream we ate some frozen pizza that Polly heated up in the toaster oven. The pizza disgusted me off and on before I finished it. This struck me as a good skill, to be able to go on eating pizza just because I told myself it was pizza even when it didn't taste or smell much like pizza. You had to be able to ride out the pockets in time when suddenly there was no bottom—no top—only strangeness. Our mother did it by telling herself that the pizza was better than usual. Hugh played chess. Our father couldn't do it at all. The Eberlanders probably threw away the pizza and ate something else. Well, actually, Iris would get sick, and Polly would be too stoned to notice. (I looked over at her while she ate and confirmed this.) It was only Charles who would throw away the pizza. The "Eberlanders" had become in some strange way just him, continually receding from the rest of us.

When the phone rang again, we were up in the library. I was staring at a framed photo of Charles, Iris, Polly, and Budge on skis. How odd that it was still up on the wall. Our father had scissored our mother out of all the old photographs in our house. But in this picture Iris had her arms around Charles's waist.

Polly was saying, "Guess what! I'm going to the movies with you," and, "Yes, I'm looking forward to it, too."

But when I got on the line, our mother said, "Aaron has already asked his roommate."

"Uh-huh," I said.

"He said yes."

Polly was making faces at me.

"Does she really want to come?" asked our mother.

"I guess so."

"I don't know what to say. It's such an honor. But maybe tonight isn't the right time. Maybe you can explain to her that Aaron and his roommate are coming."

"Aaron and his roommate are coming," I said to Polly.

"Oh, yeah?" she said.

"Of course Polly is one of my favorite people in the world . . ." Our mother trailed off.

The next time the phone rang, I answered it. "I've been thinking," said our mother. "Polly really might not have a good time. We'll probably go to a restaurant afterward, and she's used to very fancy ones."

I was getting nervous myself now, but I wasn't going to explain any of this to Polly. "What am I supposed to do?" I said.

"Don't you see what I mean?" she said. "What if she doesn't like the movie?"

I couldn't think of anything to say.

"And Iris might not want her to go."

"Do you want to talk to Polly?"

"No," she said. "I'm no good at these things. Just talk to her yourself, and see if you can make her understand."

But I took one look at Polly eating an orange and decided not to bother.

Then, when Iris came back from the office, she decided that she wanted to go to the movies, too. She said she felt so much better, she really had to get out. I got the feeling she was actually looking forward to going. For a while I hoped that Polly would object, but she didn't, so all three of us went.

The movie theater was a low brick building, slightly recessed from the other storefronts. The posters in the glass display cases were all old and yellowing, and some were torn. The movies advertised were old, too, featuring heart-stopping cherubic rebels; some were French. It looked like a very serious place—an impression heightened rather than dispelled by the Popsicle stick at the bottom of one of the cases.

The people waiting to get in looked serious, too. There were a lot of wire-rim glasses, a lot of leather purses as big as mail sacks. I caught sight of the roommate first. Because of his height, his grayish face stood out above the crowd. I could tell that the three of them had dressed up. The roommate's blue-striped dress shirt wasn't wrinkled this time. Aaron was wearing two-toned pants with dark pockets that went down to his knees. Our mother seemed to have a number of extra scarves on; certainly you didn't need scarves at head, neck, and waist all at the same time. What was funny was that Iris, in her casual clothes (open-toed espadrilles, small gold earrings, beige linen trousers), looked dressier than any of them.

I watched our mother's face change as she caught sight of Iris, recognized her, dismissed the evidence of her senses, and then realized its truth. "Iris!" she cried, brushing back at the light wispy curls of hair around her face as if clearing her eyes. "Are you dropping the girls off?"

"I occasionally go to the movies myself," said Iris.

"You mean you're coming to the movies with us!" Our mother was still astonished.

"Well, I feel so much better," said Iris, looking around. "Where's Hugh?"

"I'm so sorry he's not here," said our mother. "The first day always runs on forever."

"I hope he wasn't late getting there. We kind of lost track of the time."

I glanced at Aaron, whose eyes looked especially small and close together. "Hi, kid," he said.

"We can't cut in line," said Iris. "I don't want to shock Joan."

"What do you mean?" cried our mother.

"You never know how a person with that many ideals will react," said Iris.

"Are you sure you shouldn't be in bed?" said our mother.

Aaron raised his eyebrows at me. Iris put out her hand and then, when he didn't seem to know what to do, grabbed his and shook it. "I suppose I have to get some tickets," she said.

"Don't look at me," said Aaron, and when she'd taken off, he said, "Did you notice how she expected me to buy the tickets just because I'm a man?"

I couldn't tell whether he was serious, but our mother wasn't listening, anyway. "I really meant to get you your ticket," she said to Polly. "You must tell your mother that."

Polly clucked her tongue to indicate that this was nothing to worry about.

The movie was about two French couples. One of the wives won't have an affair with the other husband until she finds someone for her husband to have an affair with, too, so the other husband decides to interest his wife in the idea. During a particularly brightly lit scene on a beach, when towels in primary colors were moved around like playing cards, I became acutely aware that Aaron had his hand on our mother's shoulder—which was six inches away from mine—and that he was lightly stroking her upper arm. I slid down in my chair and curled my palm over the left side of my face to cut off any peripheral vision of that stroke, stroke, stroke.

Then, on the screen, one of the husbands dropped his pants, and Aaron leaned over our mother, supporting himself on her thigh, and said to me, "See that? A real man."

But our mother shushed him. "She hates people to talk in movies."

Afterward she stopped just outside the exit and suggested dinner standing amid a stream of people. Aaron and his roommate, whose name turned out to be Eddie, had already eaten; Iris said Traudy expected us to eat her chicken later; and Polly reeled off all the food we'd eaten that afternoon to prove she wasn't hungry now. Aaron said, "The munchies, huh?" and Polly glanced at him with a mild smile, as if feigning interest in something she didn't quite understand. We ended up at an Italian pastry shop.

"Pretty sexy movie, don't you think?" Aaron asked me as we sat down.

Our mother said, "I don't remember any other movie being that explicit about—which is it? Fellatio?"

"Fel-*la*-tio," said Aaron. "My God, what a word."

"That's not it?" said our mother.

"You'd think we were on Forty-second Street, the way you fling around those terms."

It was confusing, but I assumed he was being sarcastic about some presumed prissiness of hers.

Eddie had been staring at Iris since we sat down. Now he said to her, "The subtitles were very badly translated, I thought."

Iris's new slimness made her head look big, and she was wearing her thick hair waved up from her forehead, making it look even bigger. With her stiff posture, she looked like one of her campaign posters, her smallish mouth punctuated by the dot above it. She often waited a beat before responding to someone—as she was doing now—so you were hanging on her words. Yet no one was disappointed when all she said was "Oh, yes?"

Eddie nodded in a self-congratulatory fashion. "I did a half of a junior year abroad in France, you know."

"Iris has been to Europe a million times," said our mother, and Eddie said, "Of course I was immersed in the culture."

Aaron turned to me. "So what was your favorite sex scene?"

I hoped that no one would think there was a reason he was addressing such remarks to me. "I don't think I have one," I said.

"She doesn't have one!" cried Aaron.

"Well, what was yours?" asked Iris.

"I liked it when the guy gets into the girl's bed in the middle of the night and puts his dick into her and all you see is her eyes open real wide."

There was a silence.

"I understand you're an assemblywoman," said Eddie to Iris. "That must be interesting work."

His tone was so obsequious that I said, "He's a Republican."

"Oh," said Iris, startled.

That's when I felt Aaron's foot nudge up against mine. The pressure was slight enough that I didn't want to acknowledge it, so I moved just the barest fraction inside my sandal; that way he would be feeling only the edge of the leather sole, not skin.

We had our pastries by then, but instead of picking hers up to eat it, Iris was just staring down at her little plate.

"Are you all right?" said our mother.

"I'm all right," said Iris. She smiled around at the table, but then looked back at her plate again.

"Iris has had a lot of medical problems lately," said our mother.

Iris's hand flew to her breast. "I just have to be still," she said.

Everyone went quiet and watched her be still. I pressed my toes together in the silence to make my foot narrower. The strain in my toes was making my calf ache, and still Aaron's foot pressed in on me.

"Oh, no," said our mother desperately. "Should I . . . *get a cab?*"

I suddenly pressed back—hard—as if by accident, and Aaron's foot fell over. It was only his boot; he had taken it off—which made me all the madder. How slovenly, I thought. Here he was, pretending to be a hippie, and he brings along his Republican roommate.

That night in Budge's room our mother said she worried about Iris sometimes, even though she had the same doctor as the mayor. She said she thought the evening had gone pretty well, considering that Aaron was bad at handling difficult situations and that he had confessed to her he was sexually attracted to me. Then she started to undress right there in front of me. When her clothes were on, you saw the firm neck and limbs, sprinkled with those light-blond hairs that always look so girlish. You saw how slender she was. And most of all you saw the whole obscuring swirl of beads and batik, longish straight sandy hair, open-minded manner. But underneath she had a belly that lay like a hammock: wrinkled, low-slung. She said, "I think I have to buy a real nightgown to wear here." I left the room.

It's not that I had never seen this belly before. And I knew it was from Hugh and me. But I didn't want to acknowledge anything behind her youthful cover-up. I didn't want to think about her history. So I stood outside in the hall for a while, next to a string of children's hands copied in clay.

That's how I happened to hear—what? A creak? A rustle? I went to the top of the stairs and saw Iris and Traudy on the landing below. They were both slightly hunched over. Traudy was to the right of Iris, supporting her. Iris's left hand was on the bannister, squeezing. The hand seemed to get longer and skinnier as it squeezed; the shadows formed by the tendon got deeper. There was incredible tension in that hand; for a moment I thought she was trying to break the bannister. Then I noticed that she seemed to have shrunk in her clothes; her jacket looked as full as a cape. I watched the two women slowly descend the stairs, step by step. I was afraid to move. Traudy glanced back once but did not acknowledge me. They disappeared into the foyer.

In the twenty-five years since that night I have occasionally turned to our mother for help. When I was first out of college, a guy left me at a rest stop on the New Jersey Turnpike, and she was the person I called. Once I fainted at a public-policy meeting, and it was her name and number I gave to my worried co-worker. And when I finally married the man I'd been living with for ten years, she was the one who told us to buy a co-op, who gave us the down payment, and who figured out what mortgage we should get. But back when I was standing at the top of those stairs, it never even occurred to me to fetch her. All I could think of was the best way to rush down and avert disaster. I often felt I was the only person who could do this, even though I'd never really been successful at it.

I hesitated too long, however. By the time I got downstairs, no one was in the foyer, no one was in the living room, no one was in the dining room, and no one was in the kitchen. They must have left as I was on the stairs. Had I made enough noise to mask the sound of the front door opening and shutting?

I sat around in the living room for a while, but no one showed up. Then I went back up to Budge's room, where I found our mother fast asleep in a college T-shirt.

I came downstairs the next morning and found Polly sitting alone at the dining-room table, holding her hair in two pigtails on either side of her head as she stared off into space. The day was already quite hot. "Want a soda?" she said.

"A soda?" I said.

Polly raised her voice. "Traudy will treat us to sodas, won't she?"

I heard Traudy in the kitchen then, but it took her a while to appear, and when she did, she said crossly, "Aren't you going to let your cousin have any breakfast?"

Polly said, "The drugstore around the corner has the best sodas," so I said I wasn't hungry. I figured this was just a ruse to get us outside, and we'd be back before long.

"I'll pay you back," said Polly to Traudy.

"You already owe me your next week's allowance," said Traudy.

"Well, I'm bound to live into the week after that."

"Maybe," said Traudy.

It looked like neither one of them was going to mention Iris, so I asked how she was.

"She's upstairs," said Traudy. "Not seeing anyone. The doctor says, 'Stay in bed,' so what does she do? She goes to work. She goes to the *movies.*"

"She went to the emergency room last night," said Polly.

"Oh, God," I said. "What happened?"

Polly shrugged. "The same old thing," she said. "She's as crazy as a jaybird."

I was surprised. This was not the sort of thing Polly ordinarily said. Then, even though Traudy never gave her any money, we actually did go to a drugstore.

I was so surprised that I stared at the beach display in the front window as if I'd never seen one before. Hot-pink canvas chair, sunglasses on the seat, suntan lotion, a transistor radio by the crossed legs. I had never had a summer like that, and somewhere along the way I'd grown contemptuous of the whole idea. On the right as we walked in was a marble counter, about a dozen padded swivel chairs, and a long brass footrest. A teenage boy in a white uniform continued to line up soda-fountain glasses as he said, "Hey, Polly, how's your mother?"

Polly pulled a sad face and said, "You know." She sat down and pointed at me. "This is my cousin," she said.

"Joan Toolan," I said.

"Always a pleasure," he said. Now he was extracting an order pad from his shirt pocket.

"This is Richie Rich," said Polly. He showed no particular reaction to the name. "He thinks Iris is cool."

The boy nodded. He reminded me of Polly. He was handsome and all of a piece the way she was. Curly dark hair stuck out from underneath his starched white cap; his face was narrow and delicate; his arms were skinny but looked strong. He was inscrutable the way she was, too. His smiling expression was a lot like no expression at all. On the walls behind him were old-fashioned colored drawings of a hamburger, a hot dog, French fries, an ice cream cone, and a slice of pie.

"You want a Coke?" Polly asked me.

"Sure," I said.

"How about a doughnut?" said the boy. "They're fresh. Just don't get the pie. Everybody's been complaining it tastes like soap. I don't know what Slimehead was on when he made it."

I looked at Polly, who said, "Sure, we'll both have one." She twirled around on her stool a couple of times as the boy drew the sodas from the spigot. He put the glasses down in front of us, then gave us each a little white plate with a jelly doughnut in the center, and Polly pushed some bills across the table. Then she pushed a light-yellow pill over at me. I glanced again at the boy, whose face was so narrow it was almost two-dimensional. "Go ahead," said Polly, putting a pill in her own mouth.

"It says, 'Eat me,' " said the boy.

So I washed it down with soda.

"How's Dominick?" asked Polly.

"He's just as much of a pain as he ever was," said the boy. "Is there anyone he doesn't owe money to?"

The boy laughed.

So they were actually friends. This was something new. I hadn't known Polly was close to people who worked in drugstores.

"Joan's parents split up," said Polly.

"Welcome to the club," he said.

"Not a very exclusive one," I said, and then, because his smiling face didn't change, I thought a person who worked in a drugstore might have misconstrued this, so I said, "I mean, everyone's parents are divorced these days."

"Joan lives with her father, though," said Polly.

"Far out," said the boy.

"Yeah," I said.

"I haven't seen my father in two years," he said, and I felt obscurely guilty. Also, I noticed that my heart was beginning to pound faster and faster—not a pleasant sensation at all.

"Why they think we care, I don't know," said Polly.

The boy said, "Pat saw a dog sniffing around the house yesterday. We finally had to load him up with sleeping pills."

"For looking at a dog?" I said.

"There was no dog," said Polly.

I felt doubly foolish because I thought I should understand this kid better than Polly did. Shouldn't her money separate her from him irretrievably?

I began, "I don't think I can be called a Communist, exactly—" but before I could go on, Polly started to laugh and laugh, even putting her head down on the speckled counter.

"Where did you get that?" she said, finally lifting her head at me, and when her face crumpled in laughter again, I joined in, helplessly.

"What's the big joke, Richard?" This was from a thin, grizzled man in a cheap blue windbreaker who had at some point sat down in the next-to-last stool.

The boy shrugged.

"How come you rate all the pretty customers?"

"You want coffee and a doughnut?" said Richard. "Oh, hey," he said, looking at Polly, "how about pie?"

"I always have a doughnut," mused the man. "Maybe I'll have pie for a change."

We all looked at the pie under the glass. It was, after all, just a piece of pie.

Maybe it didn't really taste like soap. Richard cut a slice and put it on a thick white plate. Then we all watched the man lift the first forkful to his mouth. I could feel a sort of scared expression on my face, as if I were about to watch an animal being dissected.

The man fumbled with the first bite—perhaps from distaste, perhaps not—but he got it all down. He gave Polly a little tentative smile. Then we all watched him take a second bite.

I could tell that Richard wanted to say, "Do you like it?" but after that smile, not even he had the stomach for it. He turned his back on us to put some glasses up on a shelf covered with a folded white cloth. My heart was beating so fast I couldn't stay on the stool. I swung my arms back and forth. Polly said, "So what?" to no one in particular.

I followed her into the street. Parked in front of a broken hydrant disconsolately losing water was a red car so smooth and shiny and sleek and low it looked like it belonged under glass.

I asked Polly why she called the boy "Richie Rich."

"His name is Richard," she said.

This was probably part of her disingenuousness. Still, I was jumping out of my skin. I said, "But shouldn't he be insulted, considering you're rich, and he's not?"

Polly laughed almost as hard as she had at the drugstore. "We're not rich!" she cried. "With that drab house in Cold Spring?" She chuckled as she walked. "Besides, that house belongs to Charles now." I suppose it was the speed that was making her so cheery, but it irked me. So I stopped to read a hand-printed sign taped to a silvered street lamp, a sign that just happened to advertise a talk by a radical nun that was going to be given at a church that afternoon. I told Polly I had to go.

My heart had slowed down a little by the time I got to the church, but still I had a sort of burnt-at-the-edges feeling, especially since the church was not one of these new, oddly colored marvels with the angular architecture, but one with the traditional boxy and steepled shape. I hadn't been to a church for several years, since my new life had begun. I didn't genuflect before I entered the pew, but I had to think about it. It was much cooler than the outside. I was acutely aware of the kneelers, the missals. There were a lot more young people than there would have been at a mass, and they all filed in as if entering a regular lecture hall. A lot of non-Catholics must have found their way inside.

Sister Cathleen Kehoe spoke at a lectern to the right of the altar, next to an open-armed Virgin Mary, who was larger than she. The sister was not wearing a habit. She wore a plain dark dress and a short black cowl that allowed a bit of brown hair to show at the edges. The dress was a simpler version of something Iris would wear, as were the squarish black pumps. The sister's voice, when she started speaking of pouring blood on draft records, was almost conversational. Although she occasionally consulted notes, she seemed to be making up most of her remarks as she went along.

I was reminded of the way a certain few high school girls had looked to me when I was in junior high: serious, straight-backed, with long legs, clear skin, and an air of grace, so self-confident and aborbed in higher things (one played the violin in competitions all over New England), that they didn't look as if they could get cold or hungry or embarrassed.

Sister Cathleen Kehoe was talking about the need for civil disobedience in such mild tones that I couldn't believe anyone would disagree with her. I started to think about how much I wanted to be like her when I grew up. There was no frippery about her, but no shabbiness, either. She was streamlined; her clothes were like a habit in that they could never be inappropriate. My life would be similarly simplified, I decided, so that I could spend my time wrestling with interesting ethical questions like "Is killing ever justified?" or "Should a representative of the people do what the people want when what they want is wrong?"

The secret always seemed to be: Don't ask for too much. Nuns weren't poor; they had nothing at all. They had given all their worldly possessions to God. I would gladly have given up everything I owned (except my favorite jeans, which I would wear) to be born anew as she had been. Of course, Sister Cathleen Kehoe wasn't really a nun anymore, but I imagined her living in the same plain manner, only outside the strictures of the convent and in some free-floating forerunner of the coming society. She had, perhaps, a very small house somewhere, just a couple of rooms. She would always have exactly enough to eat—no more, no less. Meat. Vegetable. Bread. Her stomach would never gnaw with hunger. See—she did not choke on a request for donations. The need was communal, not personal.

For some reason she looked like Iris for a moment, then not. Yes, there it was again. (My heart had slowed down some, but I was getting pretty light-headed.) Neither of them seemed to have that horrible neediness on which relationships foundered. Sister Cathleen Kehoe had had a famous liaison with an activist priest who had recently been arrested. I pictured him in a group of ex-priests, all in black, all in profile, because they were always looking ahead, plotting. She would not mind that he was in jail. She would not demand too much talk and reassurance. Iris could also see someone like that now. She might meet a leading movement lawyer in Albany. Or a union organizer. We could all have dinner together. I knew such things were possible.

Traudy found me upstairs late that afternoon and said that Iris wanted to see me before it was time to go out to dinner. "You'd better not do anything to upset her," said Traudy ominously, and I nodded.

Iris was still pale and hollow-eyed, but Polly was sitting perkily on the chaise longue, tilting her head and smiling away as if she were posing for a graduation picture. Traudy stayed right next to me, as if to keep me from talking.

"I want you to be especially nice to Charles," said Iris. "It's much harder on a person to be in the wrong than to be in the right, no matter what the circumstances. Never give up the moral high ground. It is the only position of real power."

That was it. Polly gave an opaque little salute, and Traudy said, "Let's go."

The cab dropped Polly and me off in front of a white awning over a many-paned glass door. The slats between the panes, like the lettering on the awning, were gold-colored. In front of us was a woman in a thin jersey jacket with explosions of white fur at her neck and elbows.

"Eberlander," said Polly to the maître d'.

It was like no restaurant I'd ever been in. It was as quiet as a graveyard, and the maître d' spoke in such a closed-mouthed way he frightened me to death. There was too much room, really, for each table; it seemed wrong to come upon such space right off the city streets. Yet remnants of a rowdy steak house remained. There was a lot of dark paneling, the walls were painted the light burgundy of steak juice, and a waiter by a couple in the front was setting fire to a saucepan on a little folding table. Next to the saucepan was a plate with a piece of meat on it so big it hung out over the side. I hadn't had anything to eat since the doughnut at the drugstore.

Charles and Vi and Hugh were already there, in the back, under a photo of what looked like an empty boxing ring surrounded by a cheering crowd. Charles stood up as we approached, and Polly sat in the chair the maître d' pulled out for her.

"Hugh beat a master today," said Charles, settling himself so expansively he could have been sitting in an easy chair.

"It wasn't a bad game," said Hugh. For him, this was crowing.

"Are you going to be in the paper again?" asked Vi.

The prices of the food astonished me. For what a hamburger would cost, I could have bought myself another dress and maybe had enough left over for a scarf. It was really amazing that such an establishment existed in this day and age. You'd think these people would have been embarrassed, given the new consciousness awakening all over the country. One waiter brought a basket of rolls while another poured Polly and me ice water from a pewter pitcher.

"I'm glad you could come tonight instead of tomorrow," said Charles.

"We absolutely have to go to a barbecue given by one of our colleagues," said Vi. "It's business."

"Uh-huh," said Polly.

"But I was very particular about wanting holiday visits, even the Fourth of July," said Charles.

"What are you drinking?" asked Polly.

He looked down into his glass. "Why do you ask?"

"It's Scotch, of course," said Vi.

Charles looked at Polly in silence. Then he said, "If you're trying to figure out how much I've changed, I haven't."

Vi asked me how I was.

Charles continued to address Polly. "Who knows? You may even see more of me, the way things are now."

But she appeared to be deeply engrossed in the menu.

"You may get sick of me," he said with a chuckle.

"That would never happen, I assure you, Charles," said Polly.

Charles's face darkened as he said, "Don't think for one moment I've ceased being your father." Then he caught himself; he forced a smile on his face as Polly turned bright red. "I know this is all pretty strange, but you'll find that everyone is much better off now. It's when a wound is buried that it festers. Once it's out in the open air, it heals, and you can forget about it."

In the ensuing silence I remembered to put my napkin in my lap. Yet another waiter appeared, so Vi picked up a menu and said, "What are you going to have, Hugh?"

The waiter disappeared.

"How about you, Joan?"

"A steak, I guess," I said, and Vi laughed merrily. Polly shot me an unfathomable look.

"Now, let's see," said Vi. "There's the New York, the Extravaganza, the Top o' the Line, the Shell, the Forty-Niner, the Baby Cow. Any of these appeal to you?"

Polly, who had returned to her normal opaque self, said, "I'll have a salad and some onion rings, as long as they're not cooked in animal fat."

"You're not a vegetarian now," cried Vi, and Charles said, "Your mother didn't mention anything to me."

"I'm not sure she's noticed," said Polly with an injured air.

"I won't hear anything against your mother," said Charles. "She's an incredible woman."

"I just have strong views about killing," said Polly.

"Vegetarianism is a classic rejection of men," Charles said. "It's a fear of sex, a fear of birth."

"The first humans were vegetarians," said Polly.

"That's completely untrue," said Charles. "Fire was not invented to cook leaves and berries."

"Maybe they invented fire to keep warm," I said.

Neither Hugh nor I mentioned the chicken that Polly had had the night before. Hugh said, "I could eat a horse," and the two of us laughed as long as we could, which wasn't really all that long.

Polly toyed with her onion rings and ate only the cherry tomato off the top of her salad. No one could finish the steak, although Charles came close. He was the only person who had dessert.

He said, "We've finally set a date. Our wedding is going to be over Columbus Day weekend."

"It would mean everything to us if you came," said Vi. "Both of you." I didn't know who she meant by "both of you."

"Of course she's going to come," said Charles.

"Sure," said Polly. "I'll see how the older generation does it. I'm getting married myself pretty soon."

"You're what?" said Charles.

"Not right away, of course," said Polly. "I'm going to finish high school first."

Charles was still forcing a smile. "You are not going to get married when you get out of high school."

"I'm sure Richard and I are interested in a less traditional ceremony than you are, but of course I'll be able to wear white." To Vi she said, "What are you going to wear?"

"I don't think this is funny," said Charles.

"Richard wanted to ask your permission, but I told him it was no longer appropriate. We're going to write our own vows."

"*You're going to write your own vows!*" Charles said, as if this were somehow the worst news of all. "Well, we'll see about that."

"Do you love him very much?" asked Vi in sympathetic tones.

Polly started to laugh, and Vi's face fell.

"We'll pretend we never had this conversation," said Charles, summoning a waiter with his eyes.

I got the feeling Charles hadn't really believed that Polly was planning to get married. Yet she had succeeded in needling him, anyway—perhaps because he was so confused by having to control his feelings for once in his life.

As we stood up to go, the smile was back on his face. He said, "I thought I might get you your own charge card. You're old enough."

"Whatever you think is best," said Polly. "Perhaps that would be easier."

"Do you have money for a cab?"

Polly said no, although Traudy had given her more than enough when we left.

"Your poor mother," said Charles. He stopped in the center of the restaurant floor and took his wallet from his inside breast pocket as if the gesture itself were a curative one.

In the taxi, Polly said, "He is such a shithead."

"Yeah," I said, and she lit a cigarette, holding it an odd upward angle between her lips.

"No smoking in here," said the driver, and Polly said, with uncharacteristic fury, "Fine. Let me out."

We got off in a wide empty stretch of avenue next to a window display of a mannequin draped in flags. Hugh and I said nothing as Polly puffed away. Her face seemed to have gotten smaller around her tight, hard lips. At last she said bitterly, "Do you think I stuck to the 'moral high ground'?"

The next evening there was a "scratchy" dinner, a term based on something Polly had said when she was a little girl. This type of dinner wasn't really a dinner; it just meant that there was food in the refrigerator if you looked for it. I ate some sliced ham from a reclosable pack, two deviled eggs, two hamburger rolls, and a handful of iceberg lettuce. No one seemed to be around. Polly had taken out a sailboat with some former classmates early that morning, and our mother had gone off to the bank around twelve to prepare for a conference; I had spent the afternoon at a revolutionary bookstore and then a movie that was set in Mexico.

At about eight o'clock in the evening I came downstairs to "scratch" some more and found J. J. McFall alone in the living room, practicing his golf swing with an imaginary club. He stuffed his hands into his pockets when he saw me. "Hey, there," he said in his croaky voice. "I was"—he looked around—"waiting."

The question was, what for? J. J. McFall was one person I had never expected to see again. But perhaps real adults commiserated with one another when their spouses left them.

"Where is Aunt Iris?" I asked. It occurred to me that maybe I should sit down and entertain him, the way Polly would. He was still standing, but he might have been waiting for me to sit first.

"She's getting me a G and T," he said.

"A G and T," I repeated, not knowing what that was.

J.J.'s movements had a vacant look to them, as if instead of trying to move from one spot to the next, he was really just trying to get from one minute to the next. But it was hard to believe that a person dressed like that could feel a whole lot of pain. He was in crisp, light-colored chinos and a light-yellow alligator shirt—the clothes of a man about to beat someone at something. He said, "I suppose school is out."

I said that it was.

There was a pause. Then he came out with "And how is your mother?"

I said she was okay.

"She and Iris are so lucky to have each other," he said, suddenly warming to his subject. "I have a sister, but she's much older than I am. She was more of a second mother." I sat down then, and he followed suit, grasping a handful of his thigh in each hand. He said, "I'm sorry Vi and I never had kids. I always wanted to have kids."

I had been hoping to be able to keep up my end of the conversation, but I didn't know whether he was confiding in me or this was just a passing pleasantry. I said, "I wouldn't want to have kids unless I lived in a commune, where the responsibility would be shared."

"Ah," he said. "A commune."

"I don't suppose there are many here in New York."

"I wouldn't really know."

It struck me then that he had probably made his remark because he'd been thinking of me as a kid rather than as another person who could have kids. I was embarrassed, as if I'd been caught making a sexual advance. But J.J. kept sitting there, bland and distracted.

I still didn't like adults much more than our father did. It's not that I was in trouble a lot; I wasn't. I had read that a true revolutionary will obey the laws of his country in order to concentrate on his ultimate goal, despite his full realization that the laws are based on fraudulently obtained power and do not bind him. But as I got older, certain of my classmates started palling around with a few of the younger teachers—even if they weren't sleeping with them—or talking to some of the hipper parents, the kind who came to meetings on setting up a free school, say. I never did. I was comfortable with people in my grade, also with a couple of people a year ahead of me and a couple of people a year behind, but that was it.

"You know, I'd better go get myself a soda," I said, backing out of the room.

Horace was in the kitchen, saying to Iris, "I'm sorry. I'm truly sorry. But we don't get along. We never have. He gives me the creeps." He and Iris stood facing each other, quite close, except that Iris's face was turned away from him and down toward the counter, where a green glass bottle of tonic water stood.

"He's such a nice man," said Iris. "I don't know how anyone couldn't get along with him."

"His wife couldn't."

"Charles left me, too. Does that mean there's something wrong with me?"

Horace shook his shaggy gray head. "You know I don't mean that."

"Divorces aren't anyone's *fault,*" said Iris, looking over at me. "Ask Joan. She knows."

I wasn't quite sure I did know, but I stopped being invisible then, so Horace had to ask me how I was and where Polly was and all that, and eventually Iris suggested that we go up on the roof to see some fireworks that were being set off down by the river.

Except for one small wooden block intended to catch the trap door as it opened, the roof was almost completely flat, without any sort of railing or parapet at the edge. I did not venture out of the middle, but Iris did, to wave to a couple next door, who waved back with beer cans. I was reminded of rafts: All the roofs were at the same level, divided by a dark sea. Firecrackers had already started stuttering around us.

There were four folding lawn chairs, and we all sat abreast, first J.J., then Iris, then Horace, then me. Iris said to J.J., "I'm so glad you could drop by, after all. I find I'm really in the mood for company these days."

"A person thinks too much when he's alone," said Horace.

"I don't seem to think any more when I'm alone than at any other time," said J.J. "My brain just flows along like always."

I could feel Horace tense up beside me as Iris laughed.

"Where are you living now?" he asked.

"Me?" said J.J. Then, "My brother-in-law has a place in Bronxville, and I'm staying there while the family's in Italy."

"Have you seen Charles and Vi's new place?" asked Iris.

"No," said J.J.

"I already told Horace about it. It's not bad, considering it's in one of those awful postwar buildings."

I practically stopped breathing, I was so interested in this extraordinary conversation.

"There's a terrace," she said. "And they have a view of the Chrysler Building from the bathroom. You have to crane your neck, though."

"More of a glimpse than a view," said Horace.

Just then, our mother's head appeared from the floor below. Chairs had to be offered to her and refused; everyone had to be resettled (our mother on the tar paper, with her legs underneath her); she had to repeat with a perfectly straight face some excuse Hugh had given for not joining us. I was afraid that the subject of Charles and Vi's apartment would be forgotten, but Iris soon said to J.J., "I know you used to live on Park Avenue, but I never understood its appeal. We could have lived there when we were first looking around for a place. It would have been close to Charles's practice. But Brooklyn Heights was so much more adventurous."

"And you have one of the most beautiful houses I've ever seen," said our mother.

"It is fairly nice," said Iris.

This was the first time I'd ever heard this kind of interest in anyone else's life expressed here. Now that someone outside the house mattered—and mattered deeply—I could tell that this had never been true before. But the change was not necessarily for the better. Charles and Vi hadn't displayed a similar interest in Iris. Charles was just as self-enclosed as he'd ever been. I was afraid Iris's contemplation of his world instead of her own meant that she thought his was the more important one.

"It's too expensive up there," said our mother.

"It's not as if the place is very big," said Iris.

"What floor?" asked Horace.

"The fourth," said J.J., displaying the fingers on his right hand. Then, as if overwhelmed by this confidence, he rested his elbows on his knees and looked down at his feet.

There was a pause.

"So tonight's the big night," said our mother.

"What's so big about it?" I asked in a special "social" tone of voice.

Our mother said, "There's a faction at the Institute that's been trying for years to depose Charles, and now they've seized on the affair with Vi."

"Oh," I said, my voice having shrunk to size.

But Iris seemed to want to talk about this, too. "Charles thinks he can rally his forces at Dr. Tarpin's annual barbecue," she said.

"Even though he's never been to one before," said our mother. When no one reacted, she said, "Right?"

"He'll probably just lose his temper," said Iris. "But if anyone can pull it off, Charles can."

The first fireworks crackled in the sky, and a flower of red light drooped out at us. Then a huge white lacy circle peeked from behind a church spire. Some bright flashing pops lit up the smoke still left.

"I assume you'll all be attending Charles and Vi's wedding," said Iris.

"You're not going!" cried J.J., horrified.

"No, no, of course not," said Iris lightly. "I doubt they'd have the courage to invite you or me. I mean . . ." She gestured at the rest of us.

"It's going to be in some impossible place," Horace protested mildly. "I can feel it."

"No, no. It's going to be on the North Shore, maybe forty minutes outside the city," said Iris. "Fifty at the most." She displayed this acquaintance with Charles and Vi's plans as if it were the most natural thing in the world. From the street came a furious *rat-tat-tat* of firecrackers.

"I wonder if Polly is old enough to wear my blue dress," said Iris to our mother.

"Charles is a very lucky man," said J.J. quietly.

After that, no one much felt like talking for a while.

The Eberlander house had once been so swathed and coated and covered—and the fabrics had been so thick, all velvets and felts and brocades—that it had been impossible not to believe in the great importance of what was underneath. Now everything was light and airy, and I was afraid it was all going to drift away.

Psychiatrists rode the crest of cowardice that passed for being normal in the fifties. Psychiatrists were bullies dressed up in white coats. Psychiatrists made a whole science out of their sadistic impulses. Psychiatrists never cured anybody, but if their patients weren't "better" at some point, it was all the patients' fault. Psychiatrists left their wives and called it sanity. Psychiatrists were laughing all the way to the bank.

Our father would never have forbidden us to go to Charles's wedding—maybe because he knew it wouldn't work. But he was very good at keeping up this sort of bombardment. The worst part was that it got into your head; sometimes I would catch myself thinking things I'd heard him repeat over and over.

"Psy-chi-a-trists, psy-chi-a-trists" was the singsong that matched my steps as Hugh and I ran to catch a train out to the wedding. We'd had no trouble finding our way from the bus to the Long Island Rail Road, but we didn't have much time to make the connection. Hugh carried a small blue suitcase that used to be our grandmother's—she'd died a year after our mother left—and I had some jeans stuffed into a big woven purse that banged against my hip as I ran. I didn't need to carry a shirt because I was already wearing a black jersey under my dress, which was one of those gauzy, embroidered, pillowcase-shaped ones you could see through. (I was wearing black tights, too.) I wanted to slow down when the train was in sight and we could see other people walking toward it, but Hugh kept running, and some kind of panic made me run, too.

We sat down in the first seats we saw. They were across from each other; the window seats in both cases were already occupied. Hugh said, "We don't have tickets," which I managed to ignore by looking through my purse. Then he said, "I'm starving."

I grunted.

Hugh took out his pocket chess set.

I said, "I'm sure you can get the tickets on the train." My voice sounded unnatural to me, though, as if my words were an elaborate cover for a plan to slip from car to car, avoiding the conductor.

At Jamaica we switched to the train that Polly and Budge had taken out from Brooklyn. We had fourteen minutes to find them. So we went walking down the swaying aisle: faces to the left, faces to the right, faces to the left, faces to the right. Next car: faces to the left, faces to the right. All I got was a vague idea of where the bodies were positioned, in case we had to come back and sit down. So that when I did recognize Polly and Budge—in a back car—their outlines leapt out at me the way words in English do from a text printed in a foreign language.

They were sitting in a classic dreamy pose: Budge facing forward, and Polly slumped a little with her head listing slightly against the back of the seat, her face turned toward the bright countryside flashing by. They were dressed out of a storybook, in matching navy-blue maxi-coats, each with two rows of gold buttons above the high-waisted belt. I almost expected gloves. Instead, as we got closer, I could tell that Polly wasn't looking out the window, but beneath it—at a strip of metal affixed to the laminated-burlap side.

"Well, look who's here," said Budge, and Polly sat up with a start.

"What am I supposed to be doing now?" said Polly.

Budge rolled her eyes.

"I don't know," I said, as the brakes of the train squealed and huffed and hissed. I glanced around the car to see if anyone had noticed Polly, but we'd gone back far enough so that there were few people scattered about. I assumed that Polly was as high as a kite.

Budge said, "Ignore her and maybe she'll go away."

Hugh and I sat down, and Budge moved to the seat across the aisle from us. "She *wanted* to come to the wedding, you know," said Budge. "It makes you wonder what she's got up her sleeve."

"Oh," I said.

"She doesn't have a firecracker or anything in her purse, because I looked."

I glanced over at Polly again. She seemed too out of it to have any sort of scheme.

"Can you believe it? Taking a train to our own father's wedding?" said Budge.

"What's wrong with the train?" I asked.

"If his highness wouldn't drive us, her highness should have. It's all her fault, anyway."

"Vi's?" I asked.

"No—*Iris,*" said Budge.

"What do you mean?" asked Hugh, his pocket chess set abandoned on his knee. I myself was speechless, considering the circumstances under which Budge and I had parted the year before.

"She's the one who left us to become an assemblyman," said Budge. "And she's the one who said it was time to split up. I heard her."

Our station stop stood high and clean one story above the rest of the cold, gray town. Our mother, who was waiting on the platform by the stairs, waved her hand and trilled our names with equal enthusiasm. I was the one who was asked if I wanted to drive, however, and since she insisted on sitting in the backseat, she ended up with Polly, who said, "It's very wet in here." She was looking with disgust at the (perfectly ordinary) door handle.

"It's the sort of damp that gets into your bones," said our mother.

Fortunately Polly said nothing more for the rest of the drive.

From a long way off I could see what I took to be Aaron waiting in the parking lot, looking very furtive and out of place, shoulders hunched in his splintering leather jacket, the wide brim of his soft felt hat pulled low over his eyes. He studied every car that pulled in as if pricing it, before returning to his shuffling and his pacing. He had put on a lot of weight. He gestured wildly when he saw us, and yelled and pointed as I parked the car. He opened first my door, and then, without waiting for me to get out, Polly's. Polly remained immobile for a few moments. Then she said in a small voice, "Are you Aaron?"

"Whoa!" he cried. "What are *you* on?"

To get to the church, you had to come up from behind and circle around to the front on a narrow paved path. The path made a long and lazy arc, first out in the open, then amid the naked branches of some shrubs, and finally up against the woods near the door. You got the impression of space getting narrower and narrower; the church itself was small and dark and crowded. In the vestibule, as we waited for the ushers, Budge drew up so close to me that our shoulders were practically touching. Without bending her elbow, but rather leaving her arm hanging innocently straight down, she pressed some paper into my hand. "This is from Polly," she whispered. "You can have my half, too." I turned to the wall and opened my palm. In it was what was once a small square of paper with a tab of blotter acid on it. Someone had cut it in half, so that each piece of paper held half a dot. Although I'd had such things described to me, I'd never actually held one in my hand. My heart began to flutter. I slipped the papers into my purse, between the pages of a little address book I carried around, although it had only three addresses in it.

Polly and Budge were put in the first pew on the right side, and Hugh and I were put in the second, next to our mother and Aaron. There were a lot of people on Vi's side, but we were the only ones in the first two rows of Charles's. Charles had no brothers or sisters, and his parents were dead. Because the rest of the place was so crowded, I felt very much as if we were on display. Polly didn't do anything during the ceremony, though I kept thinking she might. Twice she looked blindly into the congregration, and once—more ominously—she started to laugh. But the laugh was stifled, and she was as silent as anybody during the silent parts.

Outside, afterward, when the knot of people in front of us had finally evaporated, I realized it had been part of a receiving line. There were Charles and Vi, beaming away next to the naked shrubbery. It was amazing how sunny a person Vi was. She was wearing a bright-pink suit with a big white corsage. She kissed our mother as if it were the most normal thing in the world, and our mother, kissing back, actually cried, "I'm so happy for you!" If there was an awkwardness here, I didn't sense it. Vi made everything look normal. Even Charles's odd mad-scientist brow had become a simple jutting forehead.

Now he was taking our mother's hands in both of his. He obviously valued her wholehearted approval of everything he did. He said, "How wonderful you could make it. You don't know how much it means to me." He somehow extended this to me and grabbed my hand, too. I knew he didn't like the way I dressed or talked or thought, but he always seemed to start off expecting to be pleasant to me. I smiled back at him. Then, suddenly, we were turned out of the line. I was left in mid-thought, and there was Aaron, slapping his pockets, saying, "They better be serving a real dinner."

"We've got to find Polly and Budge," said our mother anxiously. "They probably need a ride." And he said, "Not to worry. I saw them go off in a Mercedes with some gray-haired geek."

"Horace," said our mother. "I bet it was Horace."

"That I couldn't tell you," said Aaron. "So how's the chess?"

"I don't know why everyone makes such a big deal about it," said Hugh, turning away with a frown.

The reception was held in a house that was more of an idea than a residence—a vision of the future, I suppose. It was gray and spare, as purely functional as the greenhouse sloping off the back. The living room had the empty spaces and large clustered windows of an airport. In the very center were two big black leather couches set at right angles, several black leather butterfly chairs, a big square coffee table made of chrome and glass, and, on one of the glass end tables, a transparent clock. I never did learn who the place belonged to.

The food was laid out on the table in the dining room, and on the sideboard (well, I guess it was a sideboard) was a punch made from pineapple juice. I particularly noticed the punch because it was in a very fancy cut-glass bowl with matching cups; all the other plates, cups, and eating utensils were made of plastic and paper. Hugh and Aaron were two of the first people to serve themselves. Our mother suggested I talk to Aaron since he did not "mix" well. As she said this, she gave a serving spoon a vigorous shake to dislodge the coleslaw stuck there, the twist of the wrist being the same one she used to use to shake down the mercury in a thermometer. I told her I had to go to the bathroom.

I looked around for Polly and Budge, but couldn't find them. Horace didn't seem to be around, either, although quite a number of people had arrived by the time I got some food for myself: some beef fondue, various salads, and a piece of Italian bread cut on the bias. As I poured myself some punch, I was struck by how easy it would have been for Polly to spike it with acid. I knew perfectly well she hadn't done this—she hadn't even arrived, as far as I could tell—but I got a little knot in my stomach, anyway.

I sat down next to our mother on one of the leather couches in the living room. She was in a circle of women, all of them chatting and eating, mostly keeping their eyes on the plates on their knees. The oldest woman wore a knee-length navy-blue suit, and the others—maybe four or five of them—were in silk dresses. Closest to me was a pink, lavender, and lemon-yellow orchid print that was just beautiful. Our mother, too, was wearing a fairly conventional short velvet dress. I didn't particularly want to think about my own dress, but I couldn't help noticing it as I ate off my plate. It was really idiotic to have to wear a whole other set of clothes under your first layer, especially since the sweater and tights were so thick in comparison to this flimsy green thing on top.

I didn't pay much attention to what was being said until our mother introduced me. She said I just loved my cousins. The other women were all related to Vi somehow: two sisters, an aunt, a sister-in-law, a friend from college. I had no idea how our mother knew them, or how she could remember their names.

The beautiful orchid print asked me how I liked living in Brooklyn.

"I don't live in Brooklyn," I said.

This obviously made no sense to her, because she proceeded as if I hadn't said anything. "I always wondered what it would be like to grow up in the city. Polly and Budge seem to be so much more sophisticated than the girls around here."

"They've been so nice to Vi," said the orange dress with the big white dots.

"Yes—they've behaved tremendously well."

"When it comes to kids, they say a good divorce is better than a bad marriage," said the pale blue with the Buster Brown collar.

"Is that true?" our mother asked me.

She was not going to get me to okay the divorce, no matter how sensible, so I ignored her.

"The Eberlanders got the best divorce I ever saw," said the orchid print.

"I heard all four of them got together and laughed about it."

"No!" said the lime green with disbelieving delight.

"I wouldn't be surprised," said our mother.

"It's not often you get the first wife's family at the second wife's wedding," said the big white dots.

"Iris told us to come," said our mother.

"That's true," I said.

"I heard she told lots of people to come," said the orchid print.

"Iris is a very progressive person," I said. I was a little hurt to learn that her request on the roof had been a common one.

"I was at a wedding attended by the ex-wife," said our mother.

"I know of a first and second wife who exchange Christmas presents."

"Is Iris getting them a gift?" asked the pale blue.

"A *couch!*" someone cried.

It took a while for the rest of us to get this. (They're both psychiatrists, see.) And even then, as people were laughing, you could hear, "That isn't true. Is that true?"

Vi materialized by the see-through clock, but if she'd been listening, she gave no sign. She asked if anyone had seen Budge or Polly. No one had. Our mother said, "I wanted to give them a ride, but Aaron said he saw them go off with Horace."

The orchid print said, "You mean they haven't shown up?"

Our mother said, "Maybe those poor girls are still at the church. I'll never forgive myself. Shall I go look?"

"No, no," said Vi. "Charles is just impatient. I love it in him, but sometimes it can be a bit much."

As soon as she'd gone, the lime green said, "Well, my divorce was no picnic. My ex-husband transferred everything to his company's name."

"The divorce laws in this country are incredibly archaic," I said.

"Suddenly he had no assets. I was ready to kill him."

"Of course my husband came right out and said he was going to kill me," said the dark-blue suit.

"My husband said something like that, too," admitted our mother. My ears perked up here, but disbelief had become such a habit with me that I was more annoyed with her for exposing this threat to strangers than I was concerned about whether it had actually happened. "The Eberlanders are different, though," she added. "They're so . . . so glorious."

"This wedding had better be worth it, considering what they've given up," said the big dots.

"What do you mean?"

"Charles and Vi are losing their places at the Institute."

"Not necessarily," said our mother. "There's a lot going on right now, but nobody knows for sure what the outcome will be."

"I don't know where you get your information," said the dots, annoyed. "I know for a fact that it has already happened."

"I doubt the Institute wants a big scandal," our mother persisted.

"So?"

"It doesn't matter so much for Vi," said our mother, "but as president, Charles is very much in the public eye."

"Charles is in the public eye?" the other scoffed.

I didn't see how there could be amicable divorces when there weren't even amicable conversations at weddings. The knot at the bottom of my stomach had gotten worse. I put my empty plate on the coffee table and stood up as if I had a sudden purpose in mind.

I found Hugh in the kitchen, playing chess with a young man in black glasses. Given his age and sex, I didn't want to examine him too openly, but even covert glances revealed him to be very attractive, with dark, wavy hair, a long, thin nose, and a narrow chest. He and Hugh were sitting in identical positions—backs bent, shoulders hunched, heads bobbing—in matching bright-yellow director's chairs.

"Who's winning?" I asked.

Neither of them answered, but that didn't bother me. Watching chess games was something I was used to. I leaned against the counter. "Kind of hard to tell?" I said.

"He's got an interesting position," said Hugh. He was so nice I knew he was just killing time and the other guy didn't have a chance.

"Ah," I said.

Both of them wore dress shirts, but Hugh's was much thinner. And his jacket was thicker. Too flimsy, too heavy—just like my clothes.

"I wouldn't go there," said Hugh in response to one of his opponent's moves.

Hugh began to play out the consequences. The guy shook his head. "I bet you could beat nearly everyone in the Yale Chess Club," he said.

"Mmm," said Hugh.

"He already has," I said. "Or at least he beat everyone who showed up at the Open in New Haven this spring."

"Really," said the college kid, eyeing Hugh with interest.

Hugh looked up from the board. "It's just a game," he said.

This fellow was probably a junior or senior, I decided—older, anyway, than the handful of college freshmen I knew.

"Besides," I said, "you talk about people who go to Yale as if they were smarter than everyone else, when in fact they mainly just went to the right prep schools."

"I had to pass a test to get into Andover," he said.

"Really," I said with irony.

There was a silence as they went back to their game.

After a few moves, the student said, "It was pretty hard, actually."

"*You* managed to pass," I said, and then added, "I guess they didn't have a chess section."

He snorted.

The conversation did not seem to be proceeding as I'd hoped, and the next thing I knew, it was over. Charles and Vi came in and asked if anyone had seen Polly or Budge. The college kid stood up, saying, "Thank God for an excuse to end this game."

Charles said, "I suppose Horace thinks he's being funny," and Vi said, "Maybe they're lost. Did Aaron tell you which way they were going?"

I shook my head. Vi's face had taken on the self-importance that comes with a certain kind of concern.

"I'd be happy to drive you around a bit, Mr. Eberlander," said the kid, jingling some keys in his pants pocket.

"Thank you, David," said Charles. "I may take you up on that."

The newlyweds must have found Aaron next, because he came bouncing in not long afterward, holding a glass of punch over his new stomach and saying, "Whew! What a grilling. I'm glad all my neuroses are on the surface for all to see. I wouldn't want him digging into my psyche. You can't blame him, though, on a day like today." To Hugh he said, "Don't let it happen to you."

Hugh said, "Don't let what happen?"

"Marriage," said Aaron.

"I'm fourteen years old," said Hugh.

"Let's just keep it that way," said Aaron, spinning from foot to foot.

At this point the sight of him was almost welcome; at least he was familiar. The kitchen was one of those in which every surface is smooth. There were no visible knobs on the cabinets, burners on the stove, or handles on the refrigerator door.

"No one's going to get me into a monkey suit," said Aaron.

I laughed. "It's hard to believe people still do that sort of thing."

Hugh folded the board slightly and tipped the pieces into his cardboard box.

"No one's going to drag me to the altar," said Aaron. "I'm too smart. I see right through that stuff. It's just a way for women to get men to support them."

This was from a man who as far as I knew didn't even have a job. "I wouldn't worry if I were you," I said.

"I'm not talking about your mother," he said. "You don't have to get your head into a state."

"What?" I said. Hugh took off as if the conversation had nothing to do with him.

But Aaron was going on: "Marriage means a woman gets paid for having sex. You know what another word for that is? Prostitution. And that's all marriage is—prostitution." He stopped to see what effect he was having, obviously assuming that such ideas were new to me. "I don't want to shock you," he said. "I don't suppose people out there in the boonies are so honest about what's really going on between men and women."

I don't know how our mother ever had a conversation with him.

"The problem is simple," he continued. "Men want to sleep around, and women don't."

I scowled. "Men and women are exactly the same."

He looked me up and down. "You do need a little instruction, don't you?" he said. "And what have we here? A little blush? Yes! You're blushing!"

"I am not blushing," I said in confusion.

"Ha! What do you call that red in your face?"

"Just because a person doesn't want to sleep with you doesn't mean she doesn't want to sleep with anybody."

"Hey, no one's asking you," he said, suddenly wounded.

Sometime later I was standing by the bookshelves in the front of the living room eating a wedge of wedding cake and pretending to read the titles of the books stuck amid the stereo equipment and the steel figurines, when through the window I caught sight of Iris walking up the wet slate path to the front door. First, I thought I could pretend I hadn't seen her. Then I stuck my plate into the shelves at a place where the books were fairly even and hurried around to head her off.

I had seen something unusual in her face through the window, but when I opened the door I still couldn't tell what it was. She was as straight-backed and composed as ever. Maybe that was it: She was almost frozen. I stood on the threshold, staring.

"Where is she?" asked Iris.

"Where is who?" I asked fearfully.

"Polly," said Iris with a hint of irritation.

I fell back, and she pushed past me, smelling of lilacs.

"Up here." It was Horace, who was looking down from behind one of the thick white half-walls on the second floor. Even his big head was dwarfed by the size of the walls. I watched Iris glide up the gray-carpeted stairs. She joined Horace with her arms slightly raised, as if they were about to dance. Then they both disappeared behind a thick white wall to the right. From where I stood now I could see no one I knew. I sat down on a step at the bottom of the stairs.

After a while our mother appeared from above and sat down beside me, carefully pinning her knees together so no one could see up her very short dress. She said, "Apparently Polly took some LSD."

"Really?" I said.

"Budge finally admitted it. Do you know anything about how she could have gotten it?"

I said I didn't.

"I guess it's pretty easy to find at college these days. Thank God Horace was with her. I wouldn't have known where to turn."

"What did she do?"

"Well, I don't think she *did* anything."

"Oh," I said.

"But Horace knows all about drugs."

I waited a moment before saying, "Why does Horace know all about drugs?"

"Because of his friends, I guess. He's in sort of a party scene. He's a homosexual, you know."

At this I went completely silent. First I thought it was another crazy notion of our mother's and then I realized it was true. How could I not have known?

"I couldn't decide whether to stay up there," said our mother. "I want to show that I care, but I don't want to be in the way. What do you think?"

I shook my head.

We sprang up together when Charles and Iris came down the stairs, one after the other. "Have a drink while you wait," he said to her over his shoulder.

"I think I need one," said Iris, smiling down at us.

"Oh, Iris, is everything all right?" asked our mother.

"Everything's fine. Of course we're going to have a lot to talk about later." Iris was looking as good as I'd ever seen her; she had a snap in her eye and color in her cheeks. She was no longer frozen. In fact, she looked almost feverish. I recognized her red plaid kilt from years ago; even then it had been old—she'd told us she'd worn it in high school.

Our mother and I followed the two of them out to the dining room, where everybody gradually stopped talking to watch them. Charles poured some champagne. Vi brought Iris a piece of cake. "It's pretty good," she said, not letting Iris refuse it. "It's from a baker in the next town over. He's got a long waiting list. I put down our name back in, well . . ." She stopped. "Charles, why don't you get her a fork."

"My," said Iris, looking around. "What lovely champagne."

The orchid print came up to her, and the pale blue with the Buster Brown collar. Vi bustled about, picking up stray plates. Conversations in the room sparked back to life.

I went into the living room—where Budge had just started eating dinner, I noticed—found my purse, and slipped through the back to the greenhouse. I had expected exotically colored flowers, forced to bloom at unnatural times, but the plants were all green, crowded randomly onto three long plank tables. The sky was the same light gray as the cement floor. I took out one of the half tabs of acid and dissolved it on my tongue. Then I heard, "What are you eating?"

I whirled around. Sitting in a wrought-iron chair under a window cut from the original outside wall of the house was an old woman in a light-blond wig.

"Oh," I said. "Food."

"Candy?" she said.

I nodded. The wig was probably a good one, but such hair, if real, would never have been found framing such a deeply seamed face. My eyes kept trying blink away the disparity.

"Have any more?"

"No, I don't," I said, my eyes skipping from plant to plant now, wondering what was going to happen.

"I'm Vi's grandmother," she said.

I didn't introduce myself, but she didn't seem to find this odd. "Young people nowadays never stop eating," she said. "And the food! Flown in fresh from Florida, fresh from California, fresh from Peru. Do you know what a production taking a plane used to be? And now vegetables do it."

I had never done a stupider thing in my life. No one was going to drive forty minutes to rescue *me.*

"I imagine you have your own TV, your own stereo."

I watched her lift her hand. Certainly that was normal.

"Don't apologize. I'm not being critical. The more TVs, the better. Why love your misery, I always say. The world is a much, much better place now."

There: Amid the seams of her face was a lot of activity I couldn't quite pin down, as if I were looking at a drop of water under a microscope.

"Nowadays you can walk into a store and come out with a yellow tablecloth, a blue tablecloth, a checkered tablecloth, all plastic so they just wipe up. When my husband died I gave my linen tablecloths to the Salvation Army. He was very sentimentally attached to them, but he didn't have to do all the washing and ironing. Don't let anyone tell you anything else about linen. It's work, work, and more work." She shook her head. "If I weren't so old and useless, I'd invent a plastic dress."

"I think somebody did already," I said. Her wrinkles were twisting and turning like snakes, but my feet were firmer than they'd ever been: two boards stuck to the concrete floor. "I'm sorry to hear about your husband," I said.

"You're sorry he died? Well, I guess I was, too, at the time, but that was ten years ago. I should have gotten another one. Look at Vi, such a young girl, and she's already had two."

"I suppose you don't approve of divorce," I said.

"Nonsense!" she cried. "You think I disapprove of trading in husbands? Nonsense! I would have done it myself, if I could have."

As the background receded, certain objects began to reveal themselves to me: Dimensions sharpened, shadows deepened. First it was her face, then the back of the wrought-iron chair, then her wig. This was very different from opiated hash, which made everything so hazy you couldn't tell if you were actually hallucinating, or if that giant squirrel out there was just a trick of the scrim. The air was so . . . thin. It was as if I'd spent my life underwater and was just now emerging. Suddenly I knew I would be fine, and with my relief came a small disappointment.

Vi's grandmother said, "This isn't my real hair."

"Oh?" I said.

"It's a wig," she said. "No one can tell. I used to spend a lot of time and money on my hair. All that washing and setting. I was at the beauty parlor every week. I had a hairdresser named Georgia, who had a retarded boy. I forget his name; it was a very effeminate one, I thought. I would always give her an extra-big tip. Go get yourself something, I would say. She moved to San Diego eventually. I bought myself this wig two years ago. It looks better than my real hair, and I haven't gone back to a beauty parlor since. People waste a lot of time. You have to get to my age before you realize how valuable time is. I had my granddaughter's husband move my bed into the room next to the kitchen so I wouldn't spend so much time getting down the hall. A young girl like you, it doesn't matter. You run down the hall and forget what you came for, you just run back."

"Was that J.J.?" I asked. "Was it J. J. McFall who moved your bed?"

"J.J.," she said. "That's right. He was the other one. Very, very nice man. When Georgia moved to San Diego, they gave me another hairdresser—what was her name? She was much younger, with bangs that went into her eyes. She kept apologizing, because she thought I was upset about Georgia. It's true I was nervous, but at least I didn't have to leave a big tip. When I got home, I took a good long look at myself in the mirror. I never would have known that Georgia hadn't done my hair."

1971

In the spring of my senior year I went on a twenty-two-mile Hike for Hunger that was supposed to end on the plaza in Albany. Our father complained a lot, saying that whatever small contributions I could drum up would not pay for the shoe leather I was going to wear out. Allen, too, gave me a hard time, saying that these sorts of measures only delayed the revolution. A couple of other guys announced they were going to run the whole way. Fortunately, my best friend, Leila, was planning to walk with me. But I couldn't shake the fear that I was plodding through life, and then on top of everything our father got the idea that I should ask Iris to sponsor me. Generally I would ignore such suggestions until they went away, but he wouldn't let go of this one, even though I got the feeling he wasn't really serious about it. He kept needling me about my dedication to raising money for the cause. And it was true that my sponsorship was pretty meager—Leila's mother and our father himself, who would never refuse such a request in the long run but who kept his contribution to ten cents a mile. "And shoe leather!" he kept saying.

So, two days before the event, I called up Iris, who immediately offered me ten dollars a mile, thus making me—I assumed—the most well-paid hiker of the lot. "You'll have to come by to get the check," she said. And, "You couldn't have picked a better day." I would have wondered about this more if a new problem hadn't arisen: Our father suddenly offered to pick up Leila and me in Albany.

"So you can see Iris?" I said, because sometimes I could not resist seeing how far I could go.

His reply was calm, however. "Not at all," he said. "If I wanted to see Iris, all I'd have to do is call her up. We were once very good friends, you know."

"I suppose you're not going to meet me in her office," I said.

"No, I am not going to meet you in Iris's office," he said very slowly and clearly.

I didn't believe him. He may have meant what he said when he said it, but I didn't believe that had been his original intention, and I was sure he was going to change his mind again, which made me nervous. I didn't know what he'd do around Iris, or what Iris would make of him now. He had a twist to his mouth and a sidelong glitter in his eye that might have been attractive on a private detective in a movie but was less welcome on a person standing next to you.

It was warm on the day of the hike—hot in the sun. Leila and I hooked up with a kid in Hugh's class who had bushy, foot-long hair all tangled up like a thicket of weeds. For ten miles we walked along the lip of a small highway and played a game in which two of us tried to guess the third's adopted identity. Once I was a famous black revolutionary (which they got almost immediately), and another time I was Alice of *Alice's Adventures in Wonderland.* There were a few stops along the way where we rested our feet and drank oddly colored beverages loaded with electrolytes, which apparently we needed. After a while we stopped talking much at all. At fourteen miles Leila had two boomerang-shaped blisters cupping her heels, and the kid suddenly didn't feel too good, either. We all agreed that it was lucky I was the one who could go on, since I was the one generating the most money. They got a ride back from one of those parents who were always hanging around acting friendly. The last eight miles seemed twice as long as the first stretch. I walked partly alone and partly with a couple who had been together since freshman year. By the end everyone I saw had a ribbon of sunburn laid across cheeks and nose.

Then I had to walk up the steep, steep hill to the Capitol building. I almost didn't do it, it seemed so unfair. At least I did not go up the bulging steps, but went around to the side, the way everybody else did.

It made sense to me that Iris would work in a building that looked as if it belonged in Europe. It was huge; it had four big towers and lots of little ones; it was encrusted with ridges and teeth and embedded pillars. But for all this, it looked a little dingy, and the side entrance was mean and dark.

I was on my way toward it when I heard a low-pitched but penetrating "Joan!" and there was our father. He was just slamming his car door shut, trying to gesture to me at the same time. Clearly he was anxious about leaving his car even for a moment in a place where it was illegal to park. "Joan!" he said again, so I walked back to join him, and he said, "I'll be waiting right here."

"You're not coming in?" I said stupidly.

"I told you I *wasn't*," he spat out.

There was maybe ten feet of light sidewalk between us.

"What time do you want me back down here?" I asked.

"Whenever you're finished," he said.

As I pulled open one of the doors, I glanced behind me, and he was still standing there, watching.

The stairwell was huge, but dark and claustrophobic; the massive stairs were made of brownstone. There were clover leaf–shaped holes, and arches and griffins everywhere. The bulbs in the big French horn–like lamps were powerful, but the gloom was such that you could tell exactly how far the light of each extended, as if it were the dead of night. I knew I was supposed to bring Iris down. I wanted to bring Iris down. At the same time, the idea took my breath away.

I decided I'd go right in and out, but of course that wasn't possible. Iris, who was on the phone when I found her office, lifted her index finger and indicated a chair with her head. I had forgotten how exhausted I was until I sat down. I took off my sneakers and rubbed my feet. Iris's face didn't move when she was talking on the phone any more than when she was in person, but I sensed a difference in her. She was more excited than wry. Also, she'd cut her hair. The big pouf over her forehead was still there, but the back seemed to be gone. She hung up and said, "Did you survive or are you not sure yet?" And when that was dealt with, she said, "How's your father?"

"Okay," I said, panicking a little. If she'd been outside, maybe she'd seen him.

"Why don't I give you a tour?" she said, checking her watch. "There's someone I want you to see, and he won't be here for another few minutes."

I agreed, although I didn't know what I would say to any of these very busy-looking people I'd seen in the hall. I didn't know all that much about New York politics. Still, there were always larger issues to discuss.

She showed me where the Senate met, a room covered with gold leaf that looked like a huge chocolate box. Then she showed me a long green carpeted hall with velvet ropes and spidery stained-glass windows and a painting of Teddy Roosevelt. I said, "Who am I going to see?" and she said, "If I told you, it wouldn't be a surprise." She let me sit in her seat in the Assembly Room. She introduced me to a lot of people, including a representative from Suffolk County and a man who "did all the work on the mental-health bill." It was clear that she had been referring to none of them, however, and as I told them about the Hike for Hunger, I got it into my head that I was bound to meet some sort of well-known radical. Who else would she know I'd be interested in?

So when we got back to her office, and J. J. McFall was there, sitting in the chair I'd been in a half an hour earlier, I was a little annoyed. I didn't want him around when I met this person. And Iris had actually kissed J.J. and said, "I haven't told her yet," before I realized that he was the one she'd wanted me to see.

J.J., who was standing up by this point, put his arm around her, and she said, "We're getting married."

I don't think it's the young who express their emotions spontaneously—or at least not the kind of young I was. It's taken me years to learn to express a simple reaction like surprise. When I was a teenager, my first response to most everything was to shut down, to feign indifference. First I said, "Oh." But certainly this wasn't a joke. There would be no point. I rallied and said, "Congratulations," as I'd heard others do, at other times.

"I'm very much looking forward to being a member of the family," said J.J. with that raspy voice of his.

"Well, that's great," I said.

But there was something false about the tableau they formed, or maybe just something self-conscious. J.J., for all his sunny look, seemed to have disassociated himself from the arm draped across Iris's shoulders, and Iris's posture was as straight as ever.

"We're driving up to tell Polly and Budge tomorrow," she said.

They were practicing on me, I realized. "I'm sure they'll be very pleased," I said.

The conversation seemed to have stalled.

"Well, I guess it's a real surprise," said Iris.

"Are you going to live in the same house?" I asked.

She nodded. "He hid an engagement ring inside a bouquet of irises," she said.

I looked at J.J. "You did?" I said. I thought it was the dumbest thing I'd ever heard, but for some reason I was getting to like him. Arm or no arm, there he was, nodding and grinning, as full of light and movement as a carousel.

"Isn't that romantic?" said Iris.

It occurred to me then that our father might decide to find a place to park; it had been close to an hour. And when I managed to get away, I kept expecting to see him—in the narrow hallway, on the gloomy brown staircase, skulking in the shadows by the door. But he really was waiting in the car. His arm jutted out of the open window, and his hand was curled around under the roof as if it were a serving tray. He looked old.

He said nothing about how long it had been; he didn't even seem to have noticed. Instead he said, "How is she?" He started up the engine without looking at me.

"She's going to be married," I said.

He pulled into the street. "To the fellow in the gray suit?"

Dozens of men must have gone in and out of that door since I had; there was no way anyone could have picked out J.J. Still, our father acted so sure that I thought back. "He might have been wearing a gray suit," I said.

"I saw him go in with a crowd of yes-men," said our father. "He looked like a man who always got what he wanted."

"That wasn't him," I said.

"High forehead? Tortoiseshell glasses?" said our father.

"No, no."

"Kind of looked like Charles," our father persisted.

"No!" I was practically yelling.

"Well, I know what I saw," said our father. "And I didn't like it."

Next Hugh quit chess. At least I think it was then. It was a gradual process. After a while I realized I was more likely to see him reading about math than about chess. Not from a textbook, you understand, but from one of those books where half the numbers aren't real. Much later he told me he quit chess because it had made him crazy enough already, which I suppose was true. It's not something you'd have really noticed at our house.

I decided to go to Stanford the following year, because it was so far away. But after I graduated in June, I was still stuck in the Berkshires for the summer, working; my scholarship wasn't going to cover everything. I was a lifeguard at a lake about forty minutes away, a job I hated. I was always sure someone was about to drown. When our mother called to make arrangements about the Fourth of July weekend, I was annoyed she knew so little about our lives that she thought we'd be going down to Brooklyn again. I told her Hugh wasn't playing in tournaments anymore. I told her I had to work. (Hugh was working, too, of course, but he was painting houses, so he could choose his own hours.)

"Oh, no!" she wailed. "What will I tell the Eberlanders?"

I now assumed that this was her way of saying *she* was disappointed we weren't coming, and for a moment I was sorry we never told her anything.

Of course once you waver, you're lost. Iris herself called next and asked after our father, who wasn't there at the time. "Do you want me to talk to him about your coming down here?" she said.

"No, no," I said. "It isn't that."

"Did you tell him I'm going to get married again?" she asked.

It wasn't long before I was rearranging my schedule so that Hugh and I could go to New York for the weekend. We wouldn't have much time. We had to come back on Sunday, and we were supposed to get in so late Friday night our mother was in a terrible quandary. How late exactly might the bus be? And how late did the Eberlanders normally stay up? Would we wake them when we came in? Would they feel they had to ask us to wake them? After much indecision—which involved calling Massachusetts several times, despite the usual obstacles—she invited us to stay at her apartment just for the first night. But that caused new problems. She would have to buy a foldout couch. Did Hugh and I both want to sleep on it? Or should she buy two foldout chairs? She wondered what kind of finance charge there'd be if she bought on credit.

I was not getting a very welcoming feeling, and here I had traded away both my free Sundays for this one. So, although I'd been pretty monosyllabic in these conversations, I finally said with some exasperation, "Do you want us to bring sleeping bags?"

"That might be a good idea," she said. "Just in case. But maybe I could get both a foldout couch *and* a foldout chair."

Which is what she ended up doing. And although I may have been mean about it at the time, I was glad she called us back again to say we did not have to bring sleeping bags after all.

It was hot and stuffy when we arrived, even though it was ten-thirty at night. There was a musty smell everywhere, as if the entire city had been shut up in a jar for months. But our mother had also bought an air conditioner and put it in her bedroom, so the apartment had cooled off some. Sitting on the spanking new, red plush armchair and sofa—which looked very odd with all her hippie accoutrements—Hugh and I ate three different kinds of cookies. We had our choice of even more kinds of soda. Evidently she hadn't known what we'd like for our midnight snack. She couldn't have kept this stuff around normally, because everything else in her kitchen looked like bean curd.

When I awoke around noon the next day, I could hear her talking into her phone in the bedroom. I couldn't make out the words, but I could tell she was flustered, and when she heard the sudden hiss of Hugh's shower in the bathroom, she came in and said, "I always say the wrong thing."

"Oh, yeah?" I said.

"That was Iris," she explained.

"So what did you say?"

"I'm not really sure. Something about dinner last night."

"Well, you did have dinner with Charles, didn't you?"

"But she never minds that."

In years past it hadn't mattered that there really wasn't anything for us to do at the Eberlanders'. (Was there ever anything "to do," if you came right down to it?) When we stayed with them, that in itself gave our hanging around some justification, but this time our visit seemed to have no point at all.

Not that it started out that way. Dispensing with all the usual Eberlander greetings, Iris struck a high note as soon as we were in the door. "My life is like a beautiful dance," she said. "Do you see it? I switched partners in the middle, and now the dance goes on."

"What a lovely sentiment," said our mother.

Even I was surprised and pleased by this glimpse of orderliness, which soothed my mind the way a newly tidy room could. But then Iris said, "Yes, it's all worked out ideally. Which makes me wonder why Charles and Vi couldn't come to dinner tonight." Although she was addressing our mother, she looked at Polly as she continued, "I hope your memory of last night is better than the girls'. I can't get anything out of them."

Already we had been standing too long in the foyer. Our configuration had an indeterminate air. So it seemed perfectly natural when Polly simply left, saying, "I don't know what you mean," with her same old mask of innocence. Evidently her experience at the wedding hadn't changed her any.

"I had a very nice time," said our mother.

"Yes?" said Iris.

"The food was good."

"Yes, yes," said Iris. "Did Polly and Budge behave themselves?"

"Of course they did," said our mother, her eyes following Hugh as he, too, wandered off. "They have better manners than I do."

"Mmm," said Iris. "And you didn't get any idea of why Charles and Vi couldn't come to dinner tonight?"

"I didn't think to ask," said our mother.

"You weren't supposed to ask."

"Well . . ." said our mother, at a loss.

Finally I slipped away as well, but then couldn't tell why anyone else had bothered to. Polly was standing in the garden as if trying to remember where she was, and Hugh had washed up momentarily with Budge against the blue stools in the kitchen, where they were talking about sleep: "I love to sleep"; "Yeah, I could sleep all day"; "I like to stay up at night, though"; "God, that's just like me."

So I was deflected over to Traudy, who said, when I asked her how she was, "Better than some, and worse than others." She was drifting from cabinet to cabinet, putting things away in no particular order. It was as if she'd gotten smaller and smaller over the years, as people paid less attention to her, and now she was so light that any little eddy could propel her this way or that.

Budge said, "Charles is going to buy me a wide suede belt like Vi's."

Traudy said, "My Uncle Dieter's first wife showed up the morning of the day he was supposed to marry."

None of this made any sense.

"Everyone was surprised," said Traudy. "Because my Uncle Dieter's first wife had been dead for a year."

I looked at Budge and Hugh. "It was her ghost?"

"So they say," Traudy continued. "She was wearing the dress with the lace cuffs that she was buried in."

"What happened?"

"Nothing. There was no marriage. He died faithful to her memory."

"Oh," I said. Traudy's accent had become thicker as her story progressed, and I thought I'd missed something. "You mean he died that day?"

"No, no. He didn't die for years. But no one was going to marry a fellow whose first wife was on the loose like that."

Iris came in carrying a paper drinking straw, which she placed on the counter, saying, "Oh, God, not Uncle Dieter again."

Traudy pursed her lips. "You're going to have to stop buying those sesame crackers," she said. "No one here eats them."

"You forget that Charles was supposed to be here tonight."

"We must have ten boxes," said Traudy.

Our mother appeared, saying, "Charles certainly loves those crackers, doesn't he?"

"It gave him a real weight problem," said Traudy.

"Charles doesn't have a weight problem," our mother protested.

Getting stuck in the kitchen was really no better than getting stuck in the entryway, I realized. Everyone was kind of twisting around, the way objects snagged underwater do when nudged by the current.

"How's the rash?" Traudy asked Iris.

Iris rubbed her forearms, which were dotted with light-red, slightly raised patches. "I was going through Charles's stuff in the attic," she said to Hugh. "You wouldn't believe it all. I was bound to be allergic to something."

"He never threw anything away," said our mother.

"Except me?" said Iris.

"*Mother!*" wailed Budge.

"Hugh, you're a man," said Iris. "Help me understand the psychology of this. We used to be a merry foursome, Charles and Vi and J.J. and I. We were all supposed to be reunited tonight to see you people. Then Charles called up and said he wanted to take the girls out last night instead. What do you make of that?"

"Charles was going to come here?" said Hugh.

"Don't tell me you think convention is standing in his way," said Iris. (And I suppose that is what Hugh had meant.) "I certainly think we've moved beyond that, don't you?"

"Oh, yes," said our mother happily. "Charles has made a lot of progress."

"My new husband is going to be wonderful," said Iris. "It's all part of the grand design."

"Who has a design?" said Traudy.

"And everyone has been behaving splendidly," said Iris. "Don't you think?"

"Oh, Iris," said our mother. "You have the most amazing family I've ever seen."

In a way it was worse when Iris roused herself and insisted we walk to the promenade. We all had to troop off as if we had always been busy, jolly, activity-oriented sorts, although of course nothing could have been further from the truth. The streets we took were very pretty, with clean little sidewalks and slight, feathery trees fenced in by shin-high iron loops. We even cut through a cobblestone alley lined with quaint brick garages. But the heat made everything airless and unreal. I mentioned it to Budge, who said, "I know. So why did you come?"

I realized instantly that she did not mean why had I come on the walk, but why had I come to Brooklyn at all. Our conversation ceased.

The promenade was even cleaner and prettier than the streets. I leaned over the railing, pretending to be interested in the New York skyline, which erupted sudden and gigantic from the water that lay at our feet. Seagulls wheeled away from me, squawking. Then I noticed the whining streaks of cars at a curve beneath us: The promenade was built over a highway. From here it looked fast, noisy, dangerous.

Polly and Hugh, I could tell, had been flirting on the way over. (Hugh! Flirting!) I actually heard him say he had given up chess so he could have more time with his cousins. Although Polly's laugh was a bit too high and musical for my tastes, I realized it was the first I'd heard it in a long time. It made me wish I could join in, but since that was impossible, my mind soon wandered. I must have been unconsciously listening for trouble, though, because I heard our mother say, "I was so surprised to hear they were thinking of selling the house in Cold Spring."

Iris, who was sitting with her on a bench, said, "Vi wants to sell it?"

Our mother looked around as if for help. "I thought you knew."

"It will probably come to nothing." Iris still spoke coldly.

"Maybe I got it wrong."

"I assume Charles will talk her out of it," said Iris. "That house has been in the family for years."

"It's in *their* family now," Traudy pointed out.

"What family are you talking about?" said Iris. "As far as I'm concerned, that house belongs to Polly and Budge."

"That place?" said Polly. "Who wants it?" But this came off as petulance rather than humor.

Iris sighed. "I miss . . . Well, it doesn't matter." She flexed one foot, looking at her toes. "Sometimes I just miss Vi."

"Oh, Iris, maybe you can see her next week instead," said our mother, and Budge, joining me at the fence, said, "How did you stand it when your parents split up?"

She didn't seem to realize I'd frozen her out, so I said, "You get used to it after a while."

"I wish they would both die."

This is the way our father tended to talk. "You wish they'd both die?" I said. "What do you know about anything? Your parents have the ideal divorce. You can see them both. They talk all the time. They can be in the same room without killing each other." I wanted to go on; I wanted to imply horrible secrets that I'd kept back (although there were none); I was filled with passion. At the same time, however, I recognized that there was something false in this, something borrowed or only half remembered.

"Well, you live in the slums!" cried Budge.

I stared at her, speechless.

"You live in the slums!" she repeated, her face screwed up, daring me to reply.

I don't know what I would have said if I hadn't caught sight of Polly's face then. Hugh couldn't have heard—I could tell from the easy roll to his shoulders he'd have had a snappy retort—but I knew Polly had heard. Her slow, unblinking, self-contained gaze as it turned on me was even more pronounced than usual. She looked almost puzzled by the most rudimentary elements of the exchange. I found I wanted to shout at her instead of Budge.

In all the years I've known Polly since, she has never been anything but polite to me. Yet I still find her frightening in a way that Budge could never be. If Budge grew into her façade, Polly emptied out behind it, or else just froze. I saw her in Berkeley once, in the late seventies. From her address and her job—something at Big Sisters, believe it or not—I'd assumed she was leading a life somewhat like mine. But of course she wasn't, although I couldn't decide exactly where the difference lay. Certainly her denim skirt and ballet shoes were like those of half the women I knew. Yet she looked as if she'd wandered by accident into the house she was sharing. Later she didn't seem to fit any better (or worse) in any of her other incarnations, as MBA candidate, museum guide, restaurant manager, or, most often, wife. So far she has married three different men, the last of whom I actually liked, but she seemed to take them all with equally distant good grace. She has always had nice things to say about both coasts and also about the Upper Peninsula, where she lived with a fiancé who never made it to husband.

Somewhere along the way I started to notice her earrings, because they never changed, no matter what her costume. I don't mean she owned just one pair, but the spirit was the same. I never saw her in dangly hippie jewelry, or in that outsized, faux-regal stuff from the eighties. (And even *I* wore it, happily.) She wears only small pieces of gold: dots or leaves or crescent-shaped hoops. Once I admired a set of frayed-edged circles, and Polly said, "They were Mummy's." This is the sort of flat statement she makes, that could mean everything or nothing. I don't see her often enough to tell which, although I doubt more of her company would give me much of a clue. Hugh sees her every once and a while apart from weddings, but when I asked him what she meant, he said, "I think she was trying to say that the earrings were her mother's, right?" In some things he is no real use, having decided years ago to at least pretend to be happy-go-lucky.

Our mother is still unnaturally pleased when they see each other. "Guess who had lunch with Hugh yesterday!" she'll exclaim. Then she often repeats a remark Iris made during that last Fourth of July weekend, when we were on our way back from the promenade. Polly and Hugh were walking ahead of everyone else, but not so far we couldn't hear their giggling. At one point Hugh jumped up to hit at an overhanging branch, showing off a splendid long line of arm and leg. Iris caught her breath, turned to our mother, and said, "It's too bad they're cousins. Otherwise, who knows what would have happened?" It's as if they both thought there were only about ten people in the whole wide world.

In the fall I went off to California. New freshmen were met at the airport and driven in a crowded bus onto campus by way of the splendid Palm Drive. I was standing, and I was too cool to crane my neck at the mile-long passage of Canary Island date palms, but I caught glimpses. I caught enough to give my heart a little bounce. My dorm had a red tile roof, white stucco walls, a series of arched doorways—architecture for an island paradise. My roommate's family had actually spent some time on a commune in Mexico. That night I called our mother collect as promised and heard once again that Iris had loved San Francisco when she'd visited in '63. Then I called our father, who asked if I'd called our mother. A lie always feels safer than the truth, so I said, "No," and to clinch it, I added, "I called you first." But already I wasn't paying a whole lot of attention. Viewed from Palo Alto, the Berkshires and Brooklyn Heights seemed to converge, as two points always do when you move far enough away from them.

Our mother paid for my half of the telephone, and she called me every weekend. My replies were still basically monosyllabic, but there was none of the tension I'd felt when our father had been skulking nearby. I could see a couple of palm fronds and a triangle of red roof from the desk chair where I sat to talk. I learned that Charles was trying to decide where to keep the boat he'd bought for Polly and Budge that summer, that Polly hoped I would come east and go out on it, that Iris had been on it and pronounced it "spectacular." No one was going to sell the Cold Spring house—at least not yet. After a while I let it all go in one ear and out the other. I would occasionally perk up at the word "Iris," but it was hard to listen selectively. Sometimes I'd realize that I had absolutely no idea what our mother was talking about. I'd be too embarrassed to tell her, though, because I couldn't be sure she wasn't referring to something she'd mentioned the week before or even earlier in the same conversation.

The "blotches" were like that. They seemed to materialize in midair sometime early in October. It was two or three phone calls before they settled on Iris; then they got bigger, smaller, redder, paler. It was still later that they became fixed on her arms; they were the red patches I'd seen on her forearms during the summer. "O-oh," I said when I realized. Our mother of course had no idea what a leap in comprehension I'd just made. The mayor's doctor had been treating the rash, and various other symptoms, with only intermittent success. There was some talk of a wedding in November, but it was put off.

Finally our mother made a special phone call on a Wednesday to tell me a specialist had figured out Iris had a severe allergy to a mohair sweater of J.J.'s. The doctor had said that mohair was particularly allergenic, and Iris suggested that Polly, Budge, and I comb our boyfriends' closets for this fabric.

"There's not a whole lot of mohair in California," I said complacently, and then I ventured: "Did she sneeze a lot around him?"

"Oh, she's so brave about everything," our mother said vaguely.

At this point, the wedding was scheduled for early December and was to be held in the Eberlander living room. Iris was having dresses of Chinese silk made for her and Polly and Budge. They were all going to be the newly fashionable "midi" length. Our mother told me a number of times she would never give up her minis, but the next time I tuned in, her dress was also to midcalf. For a while J.J. had a plan to fill the living room with irises. His bride-to-be told him it would be impossible; she was in favor of gerberas. The champagne they were going to serve with the tea sandwiches was supposed to be so good that our mother had asked if I could try it. "It may be years before you get another chance," she said.

"Well, I am eighteen," I said. "It's perfectly legal for me to drink in New York State now."

But I still had not agreed to go back for the ceremony, even though our mother had said she would pay for the trip. In our next conversation she quoted fares and times. I noticed that a lot of this information was preceded by "Aaron says . . ." Finally I said irritably, "Why is it Aaron's place to find all this out?" and she said, a little surprised, "It's his job." Apparently Aaron had been working as a travel agent for months now. Beyond the palm fronds and the triangle of red tile you could see a perfect rhomboid of cerulean blue.

Then our mother called for a second time that week and started off by saying, "Don't worry. She's okay." A horrible, unfocused dread seized me, but it was gone in an instant: Iris had been in a minor car accident. At first our mother thought Iris's foot had been crushed, but she called me an hour later to tell me it hadn't been. It did require a cast for a month, however, and the wedding was to be put off again. I stayed in California through November, eating sweet-and-sour turkey in the dining hall for Thanksgiving with my third boyfriend of the quarter, a guy I'd met in my Marxist study group.

It occurred to me that our mother might want me to spend part of Christmas vacation with her, which I didn't really have time to do. I kept expecting her to mention it, but all she said was that she was spending the day itself as usual with Iris and her family. So when later she said I didn't know how important it was to Iris that I come to the wedding, I suddenly capitulated. I liked to think this was still code for how much our mother herself wanted me to come.

A date was set later in December, then in January. The first one I took seriously; the second one I did not. I'm not even sure why the first didn't work out—too close to the holidays, maybe. Or it might not have been a real plan; our mother could have leapt at an offhand remark of Iris's. I did not go to New York for Christmas vacation. I went to the Berkshires. Our father asked why I wasn't going to visit our mother, too, and I said I didn't feel like it. On Christmas Eve I played poker with Hugh and his friends, which I thought was fun until I realized that what looked like normal ups and downs—the gentle ebb and flow of the game—was really just me losing.

Charles gave our mother a clock with birds on it! That was what I learned Christmas Day. Also, Iris's wedding was going to be at the end of February. No mention was made of the January date. When I was back at Stanford, an invitation finally arrived on St. Valentine's Day. There was an envelope inside the envelope, and inside that was a stiff off-white card covered with a panel of unwrinkled tissue paper. Iris's wedding was going to be the first weekend in April. She told our mother that if it had to be put off again, both of her marriages might end up with the same anniversary.

Flying east for a weekend made me feel important; I got a terrific kick out of being nonchalant about it around my friends at Stanford. Being on the plane made me feel like I was really going someplace. And taking a taxi from the airport made me feel rich. But the restaurant for the rehearsal dinner was a surprise. I had been to few restaurants in my life, so there was no reason for me to be snobby about this one, but I was. Maybe it was all the stuff—ironwork, fake wood beams, nets, lanterns, views. Or maybe it was my usual inability to be impressed by anything at all.

The dinner was being held in a private room in the back. Everybody was already eating when I arrived, and the face closest to me was a stranger's. And even though the next-closest one belonged to Budge, who had a lot of "How-nice-to-see-you"s, and our mother actually stood up to exclaim over me, she also said that Hugh wasn't coming until tomorrow, which gave me an attack of loneliness. Then she said gaily, "Your father might attend the ceremony!" This was too silly to respond to, so I just sat in front of the empty plate at the end of the table. The stemmed glasses were still upside down.

The large-faced, wide-shouldered person across from me turned out to be J.J.'s sister, Ren. Her husband was on the other side of Iris and J.J. Even with these two new people, there were only eight at the dinner. It felt as if there were a lot of people missing. There was no Hugh, of course, and no Traudy, no Charles, no Aaron. The room was too big for us.

I know I must have said a few things at first, but I was feeling less and less like myself. (At college I always felt like myself, even when I was miserable.) Also, I had taken up smoking recently, and I wanted a cigarette. There was a half-empty pack in front of Ren, but I figured I could hardly light up while people were eating. I found it increasingly difficult to talk. There seemed to be nothing to grab hold of and push myself off. I spent a lot of time looking here and there, smiling blankly, pretending to listen. Whenever I was afraid Ren or Budge might ask anything more than the simplest question, I would feign interest in a conversation on the other side of the table.

When I actually focused on Iris, I noticed that her face was puffy and lined. I had always known that she was a few years older than J.J., but now she looked it. It annoyed me that I was bothered by the disparity. Certainly my attitude was a holdover from the days when the husband was supposed to be older, stronger, and more talkative than the wife. Iris was merely proving herself more radical than I.

She was saying, "When I was planning this wedding, I kept trying to figure out what went wrong with the first one. Because the kernel must have been there; I just didn't recognize it. Yet all I remember is a perfectly normal ceremony. My parents didn't really approve of Charles, but that didn't dampen my mother's enthusiasm for all the little details. We had a great time. We'd sit across from each other at the dining-room table with all our lists and fabric samples spread out around us. You were married in a church, weren't you?"

It evidently took J.J. a moment to realize she was addressing him. Then: "Oh, yes," he said.

"A nice one?"

"I'm sure it was." He shook his head. "I don't really remember."

"This food is better," said our mother, lifting her fork, and Iris, who had left most of her pasta untouched, agreed absently.

"Do you remember the way we used to eat?" our mother persisted. She couldn't have noticed anything peculiar in Iris's behavior. "I didn't have a plate of spaghetti until I was married. Then I got a recipe from *Gourmet.* I guess it wasn't too bad."

"You mean you'd never had spaghetti and meatballs!" cried Budge. "Not even as a kid!"

None of the adults had heard of cooking with garlic when they were young. No one had had a plate of lasagna before the sixties. It was a different slant on the sort of food our father got so nostalgic about.

"I can't remember whether I ended up asking Annabel to be a bridesmaid," said Iris. "I agonized about it at the time, and now it's completely slipped my mind. I hope I did."

"The girl next door?" said our mother. "I think you did."

Ren lit a cigarette, and Polly and Budge and I all followed, which gave me hope. There was always a certain camaraderie among smokers. You could talk about brands of cigarettes with anyone—a hood, an old woman on a bus, a school functionary—and feel a real kinship for maybe five minutes or so.

"There used to be endless worry about unsuitable marriages—do you remember?" said our mother. "Our parents moved us from Belmont to Lexington because a sixteen-year-old girl down the street ran off with an Italian."

J.J.'s sister Ren leaned over to get the attention of her husband. "How old was your uncle when he got married?" she yelled.

"Sixty-seven" was the husband's satisfied reply. "And his bride was thirty-three. Not bad, eh?" This last was addressed to our mother, who murmured something unfathomably enthusiastic in response.

"The marriage is still going strong," said Ren in her blaring voice. "You can't dictate terms to the human heart."

"How true," said our mother.

"She was a circus performer, a real artiste," said J.J.'s sister. "The family was stuffy about it, but they couldn't stand in the way of true love."

It occurred to me with a shock that J.J.'s family considered this impending marriage a mismatch, too, only they thought it was Iris who didn't measure up. Ren—that loud, bland Ren—was actually comparing her to a circus performer.

But Iris wasn't paying any attention, anyway. "I can't deny my past," she was saying. "I know that what's important is that I have a good man now, but I still have a whole history. It's part of me. I had one life, and now suddenly I have a different life. A much better one, that's clear, but I'm not a new person. I'm the same person I always was. That's why I don't think it's wrong to talk about my first wedding right now, even though I know it's kind of unusual." By this time, no one was looking directly at her, but down at the table, or off at a wall.

Sometimes I couldn't help but be grateful to our mother, who said, right into the pause, "Oh, Iris. You can talk about whatever you like."

"The church was so beautiful," said Iris. "It had a tiny, tiny little round window way up high, above the altar, and as the minister spoke, I kept looking up at that window and feeling as if I was getting so light with happiness, I was going to start to float up there. I guess I should have, right? I guess I should have floated away."

J.J. was taking intent, frowning sips of coffee. You could hear the lapping sounds he made with his tongue as he drank.

The top four buttons of Aaron's shirt were undone when he arrived at our mother's house the next morning, even though he was wearing his battered black leather jacket as well. He had not lost his paunch. Our mother tried to tell him that this display of chest was not appropriate for a wedding, but he seemed goaded on by her attempts at delicacy. "Why are you always telling me I'm not good enough for your precious sister?" he complained. And, "What are you afraid will happen when the others see my splendid chest?" (I, for one, kept my eyes averted.)

"Sometimes I think you try to misinterpret me," our mother said.

Outside, she tried a new tack: "Aren't you cold?"

Aaron said, "So you've got the two exes marrying each other. Very convenient. It almost makes you believe in wife-swapping."

"You have to get a wife before you can wife-swap," I pointed out.

"Send her to college, and she comes home a sophisticate," he said. I was embarrassed when I realized I was pleased.

These mixed emotions were short-lived, however. I lit a cigarette, and Aaron said, "Ho, ho, even smoking. The only problem is that you're holding your cigarette like your fingers are broken."

"You can't see my fingers from there," I said. But the remark still stung as we turned onto the Eberlanders' street.

From the sidewalk the house looked quiet and dark. There were no flowers, no paper lanterns, no lit candles—nothing to indicate that this day was any different from any other. Up closer you could see a handwritten sign on the door: "Due to an unfortunate accident, the wedding of Iris Eberlander and John James McFall has been put off until a later date. We are sorry for the inconvenience." Even the wedding invitation had used the initials "J.J."

Our mother let out the hushed, horrified "Oh, no," that I so loathed, as if whatever had happened would not have been too grave if she had not used that tone.

She knocked at first, but then soon started to pound on the door with her fists. "Maybe they're at the hospital," she said, as the house seemed shrink back from her assault. "It's me," she said to the door. "It's me."

"Maybe we should call," I said, because I generally felt I should take charge around our parents.

"Talk about cold feet," said Aaron.

Our mother opened her new purse and started to push the contents from side to side.

"What are you looking for?" I said.

"The keys," she said. "I know I transferred them." She handed me an empty glasses case with a sun woven on it and several old cosmetic cases. I was holding these when the door opened and Traudy peered out through the crack.

"I was looking for the keys," said our mother.

"I know," said Traudy, leaving me with the impression that that is why she had opened the door. Looking pointedly at Aaron, she said, "This concerns only the family."

"Of course!" cried our mother. "Aaron, you understand. I'll see you later."

"So how 'bout some lunch?" he asked me.

"I should see . . ." I trailed off vaguely.

"Come o-o-on," he drawled.

Traudy's face was shutting down, and our mother must have thought the door might be closed as well. "Aaron, go to the coffee shop on the corner," she said with a decisiveness born in desperation. "We'll see you in a minute."

We all looked at him until he said, "All right, all right," and sauntered back down the steps.

Then our mother was in the hall, crying, "Oh, Budge, what is it?" and Budge was awkwardly throwing her arms around her. They weren't much used to embracing, you could tell, but I couldn't remember the last time our mother had embraced me, and I felt stiff and cold beside them, the way I imagined Traudy always felt.

"Let's not make this Grand Central Station," Traudy said now, her mouth a line. Her dress had a thick blue brocade on the yoke, waist, and cuffs. She always wore a skirt of some kind, but there was a foreignness and a seriousness to this garment that declared it to be her wedding attire. Budge was wearing jeans.

I thought that Traudy meant we should go sit in the living room, but when I looked in I saw that folding chairs had already been set up—maybe seven or eight rows of them, with an aisle down the center. The beige couch had been pushed around in front so that it was facing out like a dais. Polly was sitting there with a cigarette in her hand. My first thought was that Iris could get married lying down.

Then Polly went through a "How nice to see you" and all that from across the expanse of chairs. I watched her stand and slowly smooth out her skirt as Traudy told us Iris had mistaken a bottle of cleaning fluid for a bottle of soda. "They're both kept in the pantry," she said. "Just one shelf away from each other."

"She mistook a bottle of cleaning fluid for a bottle of soda?" said our mother uneasily.

"Both bottles are green," said Traudy.

"You mean she drank the cleaning fluid?"

Traudy nodded.

"Oh, my God," said our mother. "Is she at the hospital?"

"She hasn't left her room. She says it's not necessary."

A silence fell over the room. Polly was still looking down at her skirt, and Budge was all white and eager, as if she were about to take a test she wasn't sure she was ready for.

"She's got all that poison in her?" said our mother.

"Well, she threw up," said Traudy. "It all happened early this morning. She drank the cleaning fluid, threw up, went to sleep, woke up a couple of hours later. Now she says she just feels a little shaky."

Budge spoke for the first time: "She said she fell asleep thinking she might never wake up again, but she didn't have the strength to call out."

What's amazing about conversations like this is that everyone continues to stand around, to take up room, to lift a hand and have it stay at the end of the wrist rather than fly off into space.

"She could be severely burned," said our mother.

No one responded.

"I mean inside."

Still no one responded.

Finally Budge said, "J.J. is upstairs talking to her."

"Through the door," said Traudy, as if to correct any mistakenly hopeful impression we may have gotten. "She won't open the bedroom door."

I'd never paid enough attention to what our mother said on the phone, but certainly I'd have noticed if she'd given any hint of this kind of trouble. How could *Iris* have done such a thing?

There was a knock on the front door, and the buzzer sounded. It was embarrassing to hear it now from the other side, to see how unwelcome it was. Polly lightly pinched back the curtain above the couch. "It's Mrs. Grue and someone else I don't recognize," she said. She was still moving very slowly—on some sort of downers, I assumed.

"They'll go away," said Budge.

"But someone has to go out and talk to these people," said Traudy in a strained voice.

"Of course," said Polly. A wide smile slowly spread across her face as she stubbed out her cigarette. She was truly scary.

We all watched her walk the wrong way down the aisle.

When she'd left, our mother said, "Iris doesn't drink soda."

She'd been addressing me—evidently to explain—but Budge was quick to protest: "She had a Dr Pepper at the awards ceremony she took me to last summer."

Traudy made a growling sound and left the room, as if all her patience had been exhausted.

I, too, left abruptly, possessed by a restlessness I hadn't experienced since our parents broke up. I couldn't bear to look at Budge's face. But when I went into the kitchen, J.J. was there, sitting slumped over by the wedding cake.

I had barely registered him before our mother was pushing past; she must have followed me. "What happened?" she said.

J.J. shrugged and shook his head.

"Should I talk to her?"

"I guess so," he said. "Someone has to."

I'd been sitting around with a bunch of other freshmen in a boy's dorm room recently when one girl—a very perky one, I could tell—had said she didn't understand why people killed themselves. Why didn't they just completely change their lives? Why didn't they go to India?

It astonished me at the time that a person could be so naïve, yet wouldn't it be wonderful if I could go up and knock on Iris's door and suggest she go to India? She could disappear into heat, sand, saris, Sivas.

Our mother was gone before I realized I was going to be left alone with J.J. Right away my breathing came awkwardly, as if I were supposed to be falling asleep in someone's arms. I tried not to move, focusing completely on one of the knobs on the cabinet doors across from me. It seemed to be slightly askew when compared with its twin. But J.J. soon said, "I know she's not going to marry me now. I know that. But if she'd given it a chance, it would have worked out fine."

"Yes," I said, nodding, glad at least to be able to look at him directly, but then shocked at what I saw: His face was knotted like a fist.

My eyes skittered away. I had been conscious of a thickness in the room, a crowding, a blocking of the light. It was from all sorts of neatly stacked bags and cartons that obviously contained the makings of a wedding. The caterers must have been caught before coming to prepare the food, but the champagne was there, and the glasses, and the silverware, and the napkins, and the two silver ice buckets, and the stack of blue-flowered serving bowls. Lying near the sink was a little white-arched bride-and-groom set—uprooted from the cake, perhaps, or never secured.

Iris had always been a person to whom many things happened. They were not all good things; what I'd heard about mainly were her trials and tribulations. But trials and tribulations are what define a romantic heroine, as long as they are endured with grace. I had assumed that the divorce would simply be another test, and at first she'd ridden the crest of it as she had everything else. When, all over the country, the new had swept out the old, she'd entered into a conspiracy of good humor with Charles. She'd even tried to prolong it by entering into what she called "the dance" with J.J. But the process of switching partners was going to be over with her wedding, and she was going to left alone with him. It must have looked to her as if she'd be be stuck with a role as second lead—as part of the other couple, the ones who got to talk to the main characters sometimes. I knew how this felt. I had felt it for years. The only shock was to realize how hard it was for Iris, too, to stay the heroine of her own life.

I tried to escape back into the living room, but stopped when I realized Budge was crying on one of the folding chairs. So I went to the bottom of the staircase. By craning my neck, I could see our mother on the landing. The top of her head and, just above it, her curled left forearm were up against Iris's bedroom door; her right hand was on the doorknob as if to take advantage of any weakening of the lock. I heard Iris say, "We no longer take it lightly."

These were crazy words—I sensed that. But her voice was distinct, measured, dry, just a little imperious—exactly as it always was. It sent a shiver up my spine. It made me rethink the other times I'd heard that voice: when she'd asked me if I'd seen our mother's apartment, when she'd talked so kindly in the library about all her injuries, when she'd told Polly and me to hold on to the moral high ground. These occasions took on a scary tilt now. And although I didn't know what she was no longer taking lightly—life? marriage?—I could not ignore the glimpse I was being given, the glimpse of something like: We will all die, we are all alone.

Our mother, when she came downstairs, was even paler than usual. Her eyes were stricken. Her light-colored hair, which stuck out here and there, looked like it was unraveling. She said, "I don't know what to do." Then she said, "Iris told me to tell you she's sorry you flew all this way for nothing."

"She still won't come out?" I said.

Our mother shook her head. "If only I'd called," she said, moving in on me. I instinctively stepped back, but she got quite close. "It's all my fault," she said.

I'd never heard her say anything like this before, and it infuriated me. As far as I was concerned, she should have had so much guilt over her own family that there wouldn't be room for any other.

"It has nothing to do with you," I said in a cutting voice.

"I should have called her this morning," she said, clamping her hands together. "I meant to."

As if her call would have distracted Iris when a wedding would not.

"I never thanked her for dinner last night." Her suffering, begging face was locked on mine. "I never do the right thing," she said softly. "Do I?"

"Just forget it," I wailed, scaring myself with all the emotion I thought I'd long since abandoned for her.

I hurried out, pretending I couldn't make Aaron wait any longer, but once outside I lingered with Polly, who said calmly, "Anyone who's coming now is late." She was looking at her watch, and I found myself looking at it, too. There were no numbers on it, only tiny flecks of gold.

"How did it go?" I said. "Did you turn everybody away?" and Polly said, "Like who?" and I said, "Like Hugh."

"Hugh never came," said Polly.

"Hunh," I said. "How about Horace?"

"Horace is in Europe," said Polly, gazing at me with that smile of hers. "Everybody was terribly unhappy he couldn't come." Her manner was so showily direct that I suspected deceit. Then I remembered how much Horace had disliked J.J.

"That's too bad," I said.

"I turned everybody away," said Polly.

We were both just sitting there on the low concrete wall of the stoop, when down the street came Hugh and our father. The familiarity of his spare silhouette was a shock. At the same time, it looked a little off, as if I were seeing him in a mirror, and everything was reversed. Hugh was rocking back and forth protectively as he walked.

"I'll get them," I said, taking off down the steps, and I heard Polly say as I went, "Tell them how happy I am to see them."

I came upon them at the end of the Eberlanders' fence and said, all in a rush, "Iris tried to kill herself by drinking cleaning fluid, and now she won't go to the hospital." All the fear and bounce and fidgets I'd been suppressing came out with this statement. In fact, I felt quiet inside for the first time since I'd arrived, now that the words were all aflutter.

But I got no answering energy from our father. He didn't dash up the steps to effect a rescue. Instead he said, "Poor Iris," and lifted the back of his hand, shaking, to his mouth. When he took it out again, I could see a curved row of bite marks.

Hugh threw me an angry look as if I were crazy myself to have blurted out such information, and I blankly registered this look a moment before I realized that I had indeed made a terrible mistake. I suppose that I must have always assumed that our father and Iris could save each other, given a chance. With a jazz song, a stinger, or a memory of tables set in tiers. Because what was needed here was not any of the normal adult coping skills our father seemed to lack so. What was needed here was a few magic words that had eluded other, more pedestrian types. But Iris and our father had had only one conversation in years. They weren't going to strike up the band now.

"I'm sorry we're late," said our father, apparently reverting to dialogue he'd originally planned. I couldn't imagine how he'd gotten so frail since Christmas. Had everything fallen apart as soon as I'd stopped paying attention?

"What's wrong with him?" I said to Hugh, because now I wanted to punish them.

This our father caught. "Why? Isn't your mother here? Am I supposed to be doing something?" he said, visibly drawing himself together.

"No," I said, backing off. "No, not at all."

Then I was afraid of being asked to go with them—of being sucked home again. But Hugh was there, of course, and he said to our father, "We'd better go."

"Yes," he said. Their imminent departure seemed to free him to speak, however, because he burst forth: "I'm sure it was the world that didn't measure up to Iris, not the other way around. Tell her I'm sorry."

"Oh, the *world,*" I said with exasperation.

The other two lingered, waiting for me to continue, but I had no idea what I wanted to say—or shout. What I really wanted to do was be very loud. And when I finally went to find Aaron at the coffee shop, I kept thinking about how wrong I'd been. If our father had gone into the brownstone, he would have been too embarrassed to talk to Iris, and Iris would have been too embarrassed to listen. Yes, they'd shared a bit of their youth—a wonderful, starry-eyed, supper-club youth—but they were also encrusted with whole adulthoods now. I might not think that should matter, but it obviously did, even on a day like today, when everyone seemed to have stepped out of his life momentarily.

Aaron was the only customer in the restaurant, and his table looked oddly empty; there was no food or even any silverware in front of him. When I sat down, I stayed sideways in the booth, my feet sticking out into the aisle.

"So who gave who the breeze?" said Aaron.

"No one gave anyone anything," I said. "Iris got sick."

"Yeah?" he said, eyeing the position I'd taken. "I see you're ready to bolt. First you make me wait all this time, and now you won't even eat with me?"

"I have to get back," I said.

"I told the waiters I was waiting for a *woman*, and now they don't know what to think," he said in a low voice.

Actually a waiter seemed to be moving quite unconcernedly in our direction, but I said in an equally low voice, "For an obnoxious person, you worry a lot about what other people think."

"Me?" he said. "I didn't just spout some nonsense about Iris Eberlander being sick."

"What do you mean?" I said. "She is sick."

"You're just a kid, you know," he said. "Even if you'd been lying your whole life, you wouldn't have had much practice."

It was ridiculous to sit here and be patronized by this jerk. Plus the idea of giving away even the small amount I knew made me nervous. But still I didn't get up. Although I would always loathe this man, I felt a certain peace, resting my eyes here and there among the three long rows of empty green-cushioned booths. He was easy—he was safe—because you didn't have to worry about hurting him. It made me think of how out of kilter our mother must feel all the time, if she found solace with him. Only she could be hurt—a small risk, compared to the disastrous consequences of her marriage.

When the waiter handed us menus, I said, "I have to go," and Aaron said, also rising, "It's just as well. You can see she's jailbait."

Back at the Eberlanders', Traudy asked me if I'd seen Budge, and I mentioned having seen her in the living room earlier.

"She's not there now," said Traudy. "And I can't find her anywhere." Her voice was strained and her forehead furrowed, as if it were really Budge that she was worried about.

Well, Budge had run away before—from Cold Spring to Brooklyn Heights. She certainly could have again. I'd often thought of running away, back when our mother had first left and things around the house had been so bad. Escape sometimes seemed as inevitable as school the next day. I was always counting and recounting my babysitting money to see if there was enough for me to take off. Now that I really had gotten away, I saw that I at least could have gone to college early. Or I could have supported myself as a waitress, given the kind of bare-bones life I was used to leading. (I couldn't believe what I was making just from waiting tables on Sunday and Monday afternoons.) And Budge probably had a lot of money to finance a getaway.

But when Budge appeared at the top of the cellar stairs, thus showing she hadn't run away, I thought that maybe I, too, had stayed at home for reasons other than lack of money. Sometimes an attraction and a repulsion are so strong you can't tell the difference between the two. Sometimes your feelings become such a thick clot you can't imagine any other place. Sometimes a sense of responsibility is so great it's as if you have to hold your breath all the time and you get relief only in quick, intermittent gasps.

Budge had probably just come from Traudy's room. There was nothing else down there, except for the storage area. But wherever she'd been, she'd done something, that was clear. She walked as if she were possessed by a decision—as if she'd crossed a line. Traudy and I followed her into the living room, where the others had gathered on the folding chairs.

"I called Daddy," said Budge.

"What did he say?" This was from our mother.

"He's coming over," said Budge.

"I'm sure she won't see *him.*" J.J.'s was a cry of hurt and disbelief.

Traudy shook her head. "It'll only make things worse."

"But he's a doctor," said our mother.

"Not the good kind," said Traudy.

I had been horrified when I learned, around the time our mother first left, how bad people were—how they would eat one another alive if they had to. It seemed to me that society had to be restructured so they couldn't. But when you took away the old bonds, people started living some twisted new unspoken version; they started to eat themselves.

When he came to the door, Charles knocked and used his key at the same time. We were all standing by then, in the space beyond the chairs, but we all just watched him come in. Already we were like bystanders crowded at an accident: disquieted, dry-eyed, ghoulish.

"She's upstairs?" said Charles, and Traudy said, "In your room," apparently unconscious of her slip.

Polly was the only one who sat down again.

Charles was up there maybe ten minutes before we heard the bedroom door open. The hinges creaked, but I think we would have sensed the opening, anyway. Perhaps the stairwell got lighter? Certainly the voices changed. The murmur was no louder and no more distinct, but it was out in the air now—you could tell. Out in the world.

Then we heard someone start down the stairs. I wasn't surprised to see Iris in Charles's arms. His face was set and hard, all his concentration on the dead weight he was supporting. She was pale and still and drooped, as if in a faint. One hand clutched his shirt placket, the gesture an avatar of desperation she was only half conscious of now. Her face, which was turned partly to his chest, was as whitely, as blankly pretty as any picture of a damsel in distress. How familiar the silhouette was—the man upright, the woman being carried, zigzag-shaped, fresh from fire or flood or savage attack. The bedroom door may have opened, but Iris's eyes were closed, sealing off the image and sealing us out. If her eyes had met anyone else's, one of us might have felt compelled to speak, and here was something finished, something complete in itself.

Traudy hurried to get the door and then backed up against the wall as Charles carried Iris out over the threshold, toward a waiting cab, back the way they must have come all those years before.

About the Author

Jacqueline Carey graduated from Swarthmore College in 1977. Stories from her collection, *Good Gossip,* appeared in *The New Yorker* and *Wigwag.* She recently left Brooklyn for Missoula, Montana, where she lives with her husband and two children.

About the Type

This book was set in Stempel Garamond, a version of a typeface originally designed by the Parisian type cutter Claude Garamond (1480–1561). The Garamond types are clear, open, and elegant.